Their eyes met on a singe of memory.

Feeling the ache of the day in his soul, Max was close enough to see the wariness in Raine's expression. "It'll be okay," he said, knowing it probably wouldn't be. "We'll get through this." Almost without thinking, he took her hands, and squeezed them when he felt the shocky cold of her skin. "I'm here for you."

I'm here for you, he'd said back at Boston General, giving her reassurance when she'd needed it, when she'd had nobody on her side. She'd leaned on him when she'd needed him, and left when she hadn't.

A familiar pattern.

He pulled his hands away abruptly and stood. "Come on," he said gruffly, more mad at himself than her. "The SUV's outside."

"What about your truck?" She stood, and the worried questions in her eyes asked about more than just the truck. *What's next? Where do we go from here?*

JESSICA ANDERSEN

UNDER THE MICROSCOPE

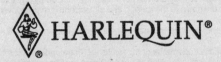

HARLEQUIN®

TORONTO • NEW YORK • LONDON
AMSTERDAM • PARIS • SYDNEY • HAMBURG
STOCKHOLM • ATHENS • TOKYO • MILAN • MADRID
PRAGUE • WARSAW • BUDAPEST • AUCKLAND

To Sally Hinkle Russell, riding coach and friend.
Thank you for everything.

ISBN-13: 978-0-373-88738-5
ISBN-10:   0-373-88738-8

UNDER THE MICROSCOPE

www.eHarlequin.com

Printed in U.S.A.

ABOUT THE AUTHOR

Though she's tried out professions ranging from cleaning sea lion cages to cloning glaucoma genes, from patent law to training horses, Jessica is happiest when she's combining all these interests with her first love: writing romances. These days she's delighted to be writing full-time on a farm in rural Connecticut that she shares with a small menagerie and a hero named Brian. She hopes you'll visit her at www.JessicaAndersen.com for info on upcoming books, contests and to say "hi"!

Books by Jessica Andersen

CAST OF CHARACTERS

Raine Montgomery—When her company's new drug, Thriller, reportedly kills four women, she must fight to prove that something—or someone—else is responsible before she becomes the next victim.

Maximilian Vasek—A private investigator specializing in medical cases, Max knows the Thriller job will propel him to the next level. But he and Raine have crossed paths before, and he doesn't trust her one bit.

Tori Campbell—Raine's assistant has the inside scoop on many things.

William Caine—Max's business partner encourages him to take the job and get Raine out of his system—one way or another.

Ike—The freelance "information specialist" is everything Raine is not—confident, sexy, self-sufficient…and Max's former lover.

Jeffrey Wells—Raine's second-in-command is her most trusted ally.

Cari Summerton—Does the young mother's death hold the key?

Prologue

Cari Summerton tucked her tiny daughter into the pink-swathed crib and whispered, "Mama and Daddy have some serious loving planned tonight."

She pressed a kiss to the sleeping baby's forehead, and felt a prickly ball of excitement just below her ribs for the first time since she'd gotten pregnant. Cari hummed as she tidied the baby's room, a saucy va-va-va-voom punctuated with a bump and grind that reminded her that she was twenty-eight, not the eighty-something she'd been feeling lately.

All that was going to change, starting tonight. She was done being depressed.

She'd vowed to remember how to be a woman, not just a mother.

The sample packet of pills hidden at the back of her closet was an important first step. Her new hair color—Sassy Strawberry—was the second; a brutal but oh-so-effective bikini wax was third; and the pièce de résistance—a naughty nightie from Victoria's Secret—was laid out on her bed amid crisp white-and-gold tissue paper.

Jimmy was due home any minute now, and tonight would be about the two of them. Nothing more, nothing less.

Still humming, Cari sashayed to the bedroom, shrugged out of the jeans and sweatshirt she thought of as her mommy uniform, and pulled the naughty nightie out of its tissue. She held it up against her body and watched her reflection in the mirror.

She looked good. She'd had a tummy tuck when the doctors had gone in for the C-section—why not?—and was toying with the idea of new breasts for her birthday. Maybe she wasn't as tight as she'd been in college, when she and Jim had met over an exploding beaker in chem lab, but she wasn't bad for a mommy.

Not a mommy, she corrected herself. Tonight was about being a woman. She rubbed her naked thighs together and her reflection smiled a secretive, satisfied moue when she pulled on the nightie. The clock clicked over to 7:35 p.m. as she draped a long silk robe over her shoulders, knowing it showed as much as it covered. Then she ducked into her closet, unearthed the hidden foil packet and pressed out one of the four pink pills the doc had given her to try.

The sweet-coated tablet went down easily, leaving her with a fizzy aftertaste, as if she'd swallowed champagne. Cari's heart beat a little faster in her chest and her blood tingled beneath her skin, revving her juices, pumping her up, making her ready for her husband. Ready for some loving.

Headlights cruised up the driveway and the automatic garage door opener cranked to life. *Jimmy!*

Her pulse stuttered as she moved through their single-level home, turning off the lights in the side rooms and dimming the kitchen chandelier to emphasize the elegant tapers she'd lit at a table set for two. Pink fizz raced through her bloodstream when the kitchen doorknob turned.

She struck a pose, feeling feminine. Feeling beautiful.

The door opened and Jimmy took one step inside before he froze and his handsome face went slack with shock. "Cari?"

Power bubbled up, stealing her breath. She shifted so the lace rode up her inner thigh. "Hey, handsome. Wanna party?"

Jimmy's carry-on hit the tile floor with a thump. Heat kindled in his green eyes and his lips lifted in a youthful smile, one that reminded her of simpler times before mortgages and college funds. He cleared his throat. "I must have made a mistake. I thought this was my house."

She laughed and crossed to him, the thrill buzzing in her veins. She reached beneath his loosened tie and unfastened the top two buttons so she could touch his dark, springy chest hair. "Let's not tell your wife, okay?"

His hands closed on her waist, seeming to burn through the layers of cloth to her core. The rasp of lace against skin was exquisite torture, and the feel of his hard body against hers was like coming home to someplace new—familiar and exciting at the same time.

"No," he said against her mouth, and his breath tasted of spearmint gum. "You're my wife. My love."

The words squeezed like a fist around her heart, reminding her that this was Jimmy, the man she'd loved pretty much since the first moment she'd seen him across the chem lab, with his eyebrows singed off. She smiled against his lips as intense, overwhelming love washed through her with the strength of an orgasm. Suddenly, breathing didn't seem so important.

Then it seemed like the most important thing in the world.

Her throat closed. Her lungs locked. There was utter, unbelievable silence in her ears, in her veins.

Heat turned to pain in an instant. *Help!*

she shrieked in her mind. *Help me!* She couldn't breathe. Couldn't speak.

Couldn't scream.

Panicked, she grabbed on to Jimmy. Pain hammered alongside the fear. Why wasn't her heart beating faster? She couldn't hear it, couldn't feel it, couldn't really feel anything. She crashed to the floor and rolled onto her back, gasping for breath that wouldn't come.

Help me!

Jimmy scrambled to her side and grabbed her arms. She saw a light flashing on the wall. He'd hit the security system panic button just inside the door.

They're on their way, she saw him mouth, and then her hearing cut back in and she heard him say, "Hang on, Cari. The paramedics will be here any minute. Just breathe. Nice and easy. Breathe!"

He'd said the same thing when she'd been in labor, but she'd been *able* to breathe then.

She struggled, head spinning, and managed to suck in half a lungful of air. She expended the precious oxygen on two words. *"The pills..."*

Then something went *boom* inside her, and everything drained away. Touch, taste, smell, everything.

The last thing to fade was the distant sound of her baby crying.

Chapter One

"Shhh! Here comes the ad." Raine Montgomery dug her manicured fingernails into her palms, trying to act boss-like when she really wanted to sing the "Hallelujah Chorus."

On the other side of the conference table sat Jeffrey Wells, the sandy-blond, baby-faced child prodigy she'd hired fresh out of grad school to help her run the company. Beside him was Tori Campbell, the thin, dark-eyed young mother Raine had hired with no secretarial references whatsoever because she'd seen too much of her old self in the woman's defeated eyes.

Taking them on had been two of the smartest decisions she'd ever made. Tori kept her organized. Jeff helped bring her visions to life.

The three leaned forward in their chairs and stared at the flat-screen TV she'd set up in the small, richly furnished conference room. As they watched, a mid-afternoon talk show cut to commercials—a household cleaner first, followed by color-enhancing shampoo. Targeted advertising, aimed straight at the prized twenty-five to fifty-something female demographic. When the screen switched from minivans to a rose-hued shot of an attractive couple, Raine swallowed against a churn of anticipation and tugged at the cowl neck of her dark blue cashmere sweater. "This is it!"

She'd seen the short advertisement a dozen times, at various points during its evolution, but watching it broadcast on national TV was different.

It was *real*.

"More than sixty million women in the U.S. suffer from libido problems," a sexy female voice said over the images of middle-aged couples holding hands. Kissing. Staring at each other over candlelit meals. The images were all clichés, but the marketing consultants had assured Raine the triteness would trigger warm, fuzzy feelings.

Damned if they weren't right, she thought, stifling a small sigh that she'd be headed home to an empty apartment after the impending office celebration wound down.

The images grew steamier, though still PG-rated. Then, the woman on the screen turned away from her partner, expression tight.

"Low libido is nothing to be ashamed of," the voice-over soothed. "Sometimes it's due to physical reasons. Other times there's no obvious cause. But this serious condition can undermine our relationships. Our self-confidence."

A small pink pill rotated on-screen as the voice said, "Now there's a new option for couples everywhere. Ask your doctor about Thriller today."

The final shot was one of lovers lying together in postcoital bliss, smiling.

But it wasn't that image—or the memory of how long it'd been since she'd experienced postcoital anything—that drove a giant lump into Raine's throat. It wasn't the sexy, feminine logo the consultants had spent six months polishing. It wasn't the short list of possible side effects—nothing worse than dizziness and insomnia—or the possible drug interaction warnings—none. It was the tiny words at the bottom of the screen.

A product of Rainey Days, Inc.

Thriller wasn't something she'd developed for her previous employer, Falco-Techno.

It was all hers.

WHEN THE TV STATION SEGUED back to the talk show, Raine hit the mute button with trembling fingers, sat for a moment and exhaled a long breath.

She'd done it.

It had taken her more than three years, but she'd done it. After leaving—okay, abandoning—her position at FalcoTechno and fleeing Boston, she'd scraped together all her money, liquidated her minimal assets, floated a few loans and used the capital to buy a drug nobody else had believed in.

She'd built a company around a dream, and it was starting to look as if that dream was becoming reality.

After three months of free sample distribution to targeted areas, Thriller would go public tomorrow. The presale numbers were already off the charts. The accounting department had even started to use the *B* word.

Blockbuster.

The experts had said it couldn't be done. They'd said the female sexual response was too complicated to reproduce in pill form.

Thankfully, all the clinical trials said the experts were wrong. Thriller worked. Women who hadn't had orgasms in years were lighting up like Christmas trees and calling for more samples with their husbands' voices in the background, urging them on. Which was a relief, as Raine had worried that men would be threatened by the little pink pills, that they would think Thriller an insult to their manhood.

But instead of saying *Our wives don't*

need that when they have us, they were saying *Give us more.*

Thank God. Raine squeezed her eyes shut and wondered if the dizziness was relief that Thriller was finally being released, or fear that the numbers wouldn't hold. If the sales didn't take off almost immediately, she'd be left swimming in debt, with a staff that needed to be paid and a slim drug portfolio that contained two flops and three promising compounds that had barely entered phase-two trials.

If Thriller tanked, it would take Rainey Days—and Raine—with it.

A hand touched her shoulder, and Tori's soft voice said, "The commercial looks fantastic. Congratulations."

The dark-haired woman slipped out of the room. The human embodiment of the word *unobtrusive,* Tori wasn't comfortable with crowds, but she gave great phone and kept Raine's professional life organized to a tee.

Jeff punched the air in victory. "That rocked!"

Raine grinned at the younger man's

enthusiasm and at the excitement that lit his mid-blue eyes. Something loosened in her chest. "Hopefully it didn't rock too hard. That's the ad targeted at our older demographic. The younger targets—music channels and some of the reality shows—will get a version that's heavier on the sex and the 'I am woman, hear me come' message."

Her face didn't heat anymore when she said stuff like that. As the Thriller mania had geared up over the past months, she'd grown used to thinking of orgasms as a marketable commodity. Jeff, on the other hand, still blushed.

The faint pink on his pale cheeks made him look younger than his twenty-three years and less worldly than his double degree would suggest. But he manned up, swallowed and nodded. "Good. That's good. You're booked on three local radio shows this week, and the Channel Four news is thinking about doing an interview. If we're lucky, that'll generate enough buzz to get you picked up by the national media."

Raine fought the wince. "Yeah, and I already know two of the interview questions, guaranteed. *Is there a personal reason you chose to develop a female sex-enhancement drug,* and the ever-popular, *have you tried it yourself?"*

The answers were no and no. She'd developed Thriller because the corresponding male sex-enhancement drug had made its parent company approximately a bazillion dollars, and she hadn't tried the product herself because, well, it was back to that whole empty-apartment thing.

She didn't have anything against dating, but she was thirty-five, divorced, childless and focused on building her company. Most of the men she met were either post-midlife crisis and looking for arm candy, or late-thirties and wanted to start a family yesterday. In the absence of someone tall, dark, handsome and not looking to sow his seed at the expense of her career, she'd decided to go with the better off alone theory.

Jeff avoided her eyes and the pink deepened. "I'm sure you'll come up with some clever answers between now and then."

"Let's brainstorm while we party. Everyone's headed to the New Bridge Tavern, right?" She could hear the muted sounds of celebration out in the main office lobby, where she'd set up another TV so the rest of her employees could watch the launch ad.

Sure, it was 3:00 p.m. on a Monday, but who really cared? They deserved to blow off some steam.

Their lives were about to change. They could bear the chilly winds of winter in New Bridge, Connecticut, long enough to walk around the corner for a party.

Jeff grinned. "That was supposed to be a surprise, boss. We thought—"

Tori burst into the room at a run. She leaned over the conference table and punched a button to activate one of the built-in phones. "You've got to hear this."

Raine grinned. "Another crank call? Something more creative than heavy breathing and fake moans?" Then she got a good look at Tori's expression and a knot formed in her stomach. "What's wrong?"

"Listen." Tori stabbed another button and cranked the speakerphone volume.

After a moment of hissing silence, her recorded voice said, "Rainey Days, Incorporated, this is Tori speaking. How may I help you?"

"Thriller killed my wife."

The oxygen evaporated from the conference room. Raine couldn't breathe. She could barely hear over the roaring in her ears.

After a long pause, Tori's voice said, "I'm sorry to hear about your wife, sir, but—"

"Cari… She had a sample packet." The man swallowed loudly, and the sound echoed on the tense air. "The doctors say she had a heart attack. She was only twenty-eight. We have a baby…."

More hissing silence.

"Oh, God. Oh, no. Nonononono—" Heart pounding, Raine looked around to see who was saying that and realized it was her. She clamped her lips together and fought the nausea. Fought the panic.

Think. She had to think.

She was in charge.

On the recording, Tori's voice said,

"Will you hold, please? I'm going to connect you to—"

There was a click, and the line went dead. After a long moment, Tori moved to punch off the speakerphone. "I called back, but nobody picked up. Caller ID says it's registered to James and Cari Summerton in Houghton, Pennsylvania, a suburb of Philly. He must've used Google to find the company and gotten the main number rather than the help line...." She trailed off. "Do you think it could be a prank?"

Raine didn't know what to think. She didn't know what to do. She could barely feel her body—everything was numb besides her brain, which pounded that same panicked litany of *no-no-no-no*.

This wasn't happening. It couldn't be.

Fear for her company bubbled up alongside basic human horror. A woman was dead. A mother.

Panic brushed at the edges of her soul, trying to take over everything, but she beat it back. She wasn't the weak woman she'd once been, ready to crumble and let someone else take over and fix things. She couldn't be.

She was the boss now.

She placed her palms flat on the conference table and pressed until the numbness receded and she could feel the wood grain beneath her fingertips. "Cancel the party. We have work to do."

THAT NIGHT, RAINE SLEPT a couple of hours stretched out on the couch in her office, waiting for new information. She had to have new information because what little they had didn't make an iota of sense.

Thriller hadn't killed Cari Summerton. It couldn't have.

The fast-track clinical trials had shown that it was safe for human use. The toxicities were so minor as to be nonexistent. The drug researchers hadn't noted anything unexpected—certainly nothing had suggested a connection between Thriller and heart attacks. There had to be another explanation for the woman's death.

But what, exactly?

Coincidence? Fraud? Something else?

As the cold winter dawn broke outside her office window, her mind buzzed with the possibilities, each of which seemed equally unlikely, but none more unlikely— at least to her—than the thought that her drug was a killer.

Please, God, let there be another explanation.

By ten that morning, as Raine downed her third cup of coffee, changed into the spare power suit she kept in the office closet and headed for a council of war, she wasn't any closer to an answer. She just hoped to hell they found one soon.

Tension hung heavy in the conference room, which was crammed with nearly half of Raine's forty-person staff. She sat at the head of the table and gestured for Jeff to begin with the first report. "What have we got on the caller? Is James Summerton for real?"

A sleepless night was etched in the young man's earnest face, but he shook his head. "Not much. I've confirmed the names and the address, but nobody's answering the phone. I can't find an obituary on Cari Summerton in the local paper, but they may not have gotten it organized yet." He paused. "Sorry. I wish I had more for you."

So do I, Raine thought, but she didn't say it aloud because she knew Jeff was already working as hard as he could. They'd each taken a chance on the other—her in hiring a young genius with no managerial experience, him in working for a startup company with only one major product in the pipeline. He was putting his sickly younger brother through college. She was trying to grow up at the age of thirty-five and learn how to take charge of her own life.

They both needed Thriller to succeed.

"Keep looking," she said. "We need to be absolutely certain this guy is for real before we proceed." Scam artists had planted severed fingers in fast food before, looking for a quick settlement. It was possible that Summerton was looking to cash in on an unexpected—or faked—death, figuring the company would pay rather than risk Thriller's reputation on the eve of its launch.

If that was the case, she'd be tempted to

pay, just to keep things quiet. But, if there *was* a problem with Thriller, they needed to know about it before the drug went on sale. She was trying to do this right, trying to protect the consumer while covering her own butt.

She had already called the Food and Drug Administration—FDA—where she'd filed an unexpected toxicity report that likely wouldn't get read for a few days or even a week. Then she'd called her distributors, delaying the launch.

She'd said there were problems with the print ads and the commercials, that the hype wasn't where she needed it to be. "Push it back a week," she'd said. "We'll have everything straightened out by then."

She hoped.

That had taken care of the new prescriptions, but there were thousands of sample packets already in use. Were they safe or not? One possibly fraudulent death report wasn't sufficient evidence for her to recall the samples, but if another user died and the press got wind that Rainey Days had known about the problem…

Instant media crisis. How could she balance the company's welfare against the possibility that she might be endangering lives?

Raine pinched the bridge of her nose, trying to fight back the impending headache. She gestured to her head epidemiologist, Red, who was a sharp-faced woman with wild auburn hair, a mercurial temper and a photographic recall for facts and figures. Raine asked, "Did your department find any cardiac problems in the toxicity databases?"

Red scowled, apparently taking the question—and the death—as a personal affront. "Of course not. There's nothing to find. Thriller is safe for human use. Hell, it scores better in terms of side effects and cross-reactions than *aspirin*. This is a set-up. It has to be."

Raine, who'd butted heads with Red on more than one occasion, fixed her with a stern look. "You *did* check the clinical-trial databases for cardiac toxicity reports, right?"

The epidemiologist bristled. "Of course.

There were none. Headaches. Sleeplessness. A few sniffles. Nothing more, like I already told you six times."

Ignoring the attitude because Red was the best at what she did, personal style notwithstanding, Raine called on the other department heads. They didn't have much to add until she reached Phillip Worth, the gaunt, forty-something head of the legal department.

"You need to get yourself an investigator," Phil said. "We can't plan a strategy without more information. Is the dead woman really dead? Did she actually take Thriller? Was an autopsy performed? Tox screen?" He spread his hands. "There'll either be a monetary demand or a lawsuit. We need to be prepared for both."

Raine nodded. "You're right. I know you're right." Both about the preparations and the investigator. "I'll work on it."

She dismissed the meeting soon after, knowing that the longer they sat there, the more unanswered questions they'd accumulate.

Tori lingered while the others filed out.

She was quiet for a moment, then said, "What's wrong?"

Raine nearly laughed because at this point what *wasn't* wrong? But she knew that wasn't what Tori was asking.

The women weren't close, weren't even really friends, but they shared an unspoken bond of two people working to figure out who they were when everyone around them had been defining them for too long.

Tori had an ex-husband with quick fists. Raine didn't have that excuse.

Aware that her receptionist was waiting for an answer, Raine blew out a breath. "There are three major pharmaceutical investigation firms in the northeast. The top two won't take the case without a six-figure retainer." She dug her nails into her palms and felt success trickling away. "Everything I have—and then some—is tied up in Thriller. I had to borrow against the office computers to pay for the TV spots."

Saying it aloud only made it sound worse.

"You said there were three companies. What about the third?"

"Vasek and Caine Investigations," Raine said, trying to ignore the fine buzz of warmth that ran through her when she said the name. "It's a small company, fairly new, but it's gotten a hell of a cachet in the past few years. They have the reputation of taking on the impossible cases and making them possible."

Tori's eyes narrowed and she studied Raine's face. "Which one are you avoiding, Vasek or Caine?"

. Raine winced. "That would be Maximilian Vasek. Max. We had a…"

She wasn't even sure what to call it. They hadn't dated, hadn't been lovers, hadn't even kissed. He had known her during the worst weeks of her life, three years earlier. She'd leaned on him, depended on him, formed a connection with him.

And then she'd taken off.

She hadn't even said goodbye. She hadn't known how to.

"We knew each other," she said finally. "It didn't end well."

"Did it end badly enough that he'd turn

you down flat if you called and explained the situation?" Tori asked.

"I don't know." It was possible the emotion had been all on her side, that he'd been relieved when she left. And hell, it'd been three years. Surely she was little more than a bad memory by now?

Surely, he didn't still think of her, didn't still wonder what might have happened if she'd stayed and worked through her problems back in Boston rather than running away?

"Call him," Tori ordered, sounding bossier than Raine had ever heard her before.

"There's got to be something else we can try first." Raine heard a pleading note creep into her voice. She'd stared at the New York phone number off and on all morning, knowing she had to make the call.

She wasn't sure which would be worse— having him hang up on her, or having him not remember her at all. In fact, it would probably be better just to show up. He wouldn't throw her out of the office.

Would he?

A knock brought Raine's head up in time to see Jeff enter the room. His expression was grim enough to send a chill racing across her skin when he said, "You need to see this."

He clicked on the TV, the one they'd used to watch the debut of her commercial—was it only yesterday? It felt like a week ago.

He tuned to one of the major twenty-four-hour news stations, and Raine's stomach knotted. "Oh, God. Cari Summerton's family went public?"

If they had, it meant this wasn't a scam. There really was a dead woman. She really had taken Thriller. Those basic facts were too easy for the reporters to check.

It also meant the media bloodbath had begun.

Jeff shook his head, eyes hollow. "Worse. Whoever broke the story got three other families to come forward. It's not just one dead woman, it's four."

Four dead.

The words buzzed in Raine's brain like a scream that was echoed in the strident ring of the conference-room phone. Tori answered, and her already pale face went ghost-white. "Please hold."

She held the receiver out to Raine just as the TV news crawl read, *Four women die after taking the sex-enhancement drug Thriller. A spokesperson for the Food and Drug Administration reports that an investigation will be launched immediately.*

Raine looked at the handset. "Is that the FDA?" When Tori nodded, Raine pinched the bridge of her nose, where a stress headache had taken up permanent residence. "I guess it's time for that last resort."

It looked like she was headed to New York.

And Max.

Chapter Two

When a knock at the apartment door signaled the arrival of his take-out dinner, Max Vasek poked his head out of the bathroom and yelled, "Be right there!"

And it was about time, too. He'd called in the order nearly forty minutes ago. Then again, he'd learned that stuff like deliveries and repairs always took twice as long in New York City versus back in Boston, where he'd grown up and spent a chunk of his adult life.

It was a geographic law or something.

Hair still damp from his post-gym shower, wearing worn jeans and a heavy flannel shirt he'd left unbuttoned because the thermostat was on the fritz again and the five-room apartment was randomly cycling between arctic and parboil, Max padded to the door barefoot. He plucked a ten and a twenty from his wallet, undid the safety locks and opened the door. "Keep the—"

Then he stopped. Standing outside his apartment was a tall woman wearing a calf-length red coat and a bulky wool hat, tipped down so it obscured her face. She was long and lean, with a big leather bag slung diagonally across her body, city-style.

Clearly not his Chinese food.

"Whoops, sorry." Max rocked back on his heels. "You the new tenant in 5B? If you're wondering about the heat, the super said he'd get to it this week sometime, and he's pretty good about stuff like that."

The woman took a breath, and he saw her gloved hands twine together and hold before she said, "I'm not the new tenant." Her husky voice was the first punch of a one-two, with "two" following the moment she looked up, so he could see her face. "I need to talk to you."

Max's breath whistled between his teeth, forced by the shock of that second punch.

Her long dark hair was pulled back under her hat, but a few loose curls touched the aristocratic angles of her face and the long curve of her neck. Her eyes were a haunting light brown that seemed to glow against her rosy skin and dark lashes, adding a pout to her full, dusky lips.

Raine Montgomery. He knew her instantly, even after—what had it been? Two years? Three?

Three years since she'd disappeared from her room at Boston General Hospital without a word, proving that he'd been wrong about her. She hadn't had a deeper layer buried beneath the brittle, scared exterior. She had been exactly what she'd seemed on the surface. Shallow. Self-absorbed. Career-minded at the expense of family or loyalty.

And so achingly beautiful he'd talked himself into believing she needed him, talked himself into believing they had a future together.

Until she'd taken off.

"I went to your office and spoke with your partner. He gave me this address. I hope you don't mind." She tilted her head to look up at him, because although she was a slender five foot ten, he still topped her by nearly six inches. "May I come in?"

"I do mind." In fact, he was going to kill William for giving out his home address. "And no, you can't come in." Max didn't need to glance back into the bare rooms to know he didn't want her anywhere near his apartment, or his life. "Since I know damn well this isn't a social call, I can only assume you have a case for Vasek and Caine. Make an appointment during business hours and we'll see what we can do for you."

Translation: he'd pawn her off on William, who was nearly impervious to big brown eyes.

Max was tempted to tell her to get lost, but he wasn't an idiot. He knew her company was getting set to launch their highly touted female sex-enhancement drug—not because he'd been keeping tabs on her, but because the buzz had been impossible to ignore. It stood to reason that she wanted to see him about Thriller.

The drug was slated to bring in big money. Big publicity. Exactly the sort of thing his and William's company needed if they wanted to break out of the nickel-and-dime stuff and into mainstream competition.

"Tomorrow could be too late," she argued. "I need to talk to you now."

He was faintly surprised by the persistence, which jarred against his memory of a quiet, polite woman in a hospital bed, one who didn't want to be fussed over as the doctors struggled to control a blood clotting issue. It was that very desire not to make a fuss that had made him want to fuss over her. Want to be with her. Want to wrap her in silk and take her away from danger and ugliness.

It was what his techie friend Ike called DIDS. Damsel In Distress Syndrome.

But, Max thought grimly, *knowing you have a problem is the first step in fighting it.*

He didn't budge from the door. "You need to talk to me? So talk."

She took a breath and glanced away. "First, I need to apologize. You were nothing but kind to me three years ago, and I treated you badly. I was sick, hormonal and upset and going through a really terrible time in my life, but that's no excuse." She paused and looked at him squarely before she said, "I'm sorry. I should have said goodbye."

Three years ago, that might have mattered to him.

Now, he scowled. "Agreed. So what?"

He expected her to back down. Instead, she stood her ground while something dark and haunted moved through her expression. "I'm in trouble. You've heard of Thriller?"

He nodded, accepting the change of topic if not the apology. "Female sexuality drug. Lots of publicity. Launches sometime this week."

"Actually, it was supposed to launch today. The FDA put a hold on it." Still standing in the hallway, she unslung the leather bag from around her neck, opened it and pulled out a folder that was filled with a half inch of papers and had a data disk taped to the front inside a plastic sleeve. She offered it to him. "Four women are dead from cardiac arrest. According to the reports, the only thing they had in common was that all four took Thriller before they died."

He ignored the folder. "Call William in the morning and make an appointment. Our history back in Boston doesn't give you the right to hunt me up at home, and it doesn't qualify you for preferential treatment. Hell, if anything, I should tell him to ask for hazard pay."

He told himself he'd meant the comment as a joke, but it landed flat.

Three years earlier, he'd been more or less content with his lab work at Boston General Hospital. With a Ph.D in biochemistry, a postdoc in a fertility lab and a half-dozen major first-author papers to his name, he could've run his own group, but preferred having someone else manage the basics, leaving him free to pursue interesting side projects.

It was one such side project that had

put him in contact with a then-pregnant Raine. When danger had stalked the lab and its patients, Max had appointed himself the pretty divorcée's guardian, and had thought his growing feelings were reciprocated.

In the end, an empty hospital room had proven otherwise.

"I already spoke to your partner about the case," she said quickly. "He told me to talk to you."

Max bet she was leaving out a few steps. Like how she'd conned William into giving up his address. No doubt she'd implied— or outright said—that they'd been lovers, when they'd been nothing of the sort.

Though they might have been lovers. If they'd met at another time, under different circumstances…

It didn't matter, Max told himself. They'd met the way they'd met, and parted the way they'd parted.

And he'd gone on to make some really bad decisions in the aftermath. Maybe it wasn't fair to blame her for them, but that didn't change the upshot.

Damsels in distress were nothing but trouble.

He held up a hand before she could speak again. "Look, Raine. An apology doesn't change anything." He stepped back, into the apartment. "If you want Vasek and Caine to handle your case, you'll have to deal with William, not me."

With that, he shut the door on her. He didn't slam it, because a slam would indicate anger, suggesting he still cared.

No, he shut it gently, with a firm, final-sounding *thunk*.

Then he locked and double locked it. But as he turned away from the door and stared into the barren apartment, which had been stripped of most of its furnishings and absolutely everything of monetary value, he had to wonder.

Was he locking her out, or locking himself in?

RAINE STOOD IN THE HALLWAY for a long moment, trembling. Not with fear or anger, though that was part of it. And not with the accumulated stress of the past two days, though that was part of it, too. But the rest of it was Max.

She'd thought she'd been prepared to see him.

She'd been wrong.

He was taller than she remembered, and broader, but his voice was the same, a deep, dark rumble that used an educated man's vocabulary in a blue-collar Boston accent. His face remained a collection of heavy planes and angles that shouldn't have been handsome but somehow was, even beneath a faint shadow of stubble. All that was the same.

But his eyes were different. How he'd looked at her was different.

When they'd known each other for those few short weeks at Boston General, under the strangest of circumstances, he'd treated her so kindly, so gently. He hadn't said much, but he'd been there through the entire terrifying ordeal, and he'd never looked at her as though she were the enemy, as though she had betrayed him.

Never looked at her the way he had just now.

"It's nothing more than I deserve," she said aloud. "I took off on him."

It occurred to her that his reaction—along with his partner's raised brows and quick cooperation when she'd given her name—was confirmation that Max remembered her, evidence that the feelings hadn't been all on her side. But it was also proof that she'd hurt him when she'd left, and she hadn't wanted that.

She'd wanted to punish herself for getting sick and miscarrying the baby, not him. But it seemed as though she'd managed to do both, and she wasn't sure how to fix it. Wasn't sure it was fixable at all.

On the long, traffic-delayed drive from the Vasek and Caine offices in Manhattan, she'd worked out what she would say when Max opened the door. But the shock of seeing him had driven the planned speech out of her head.

He'd turned her down before she'd been able to get back on track. So now what?

"General Gao's?"

Raine gasped and spun at the unfamiliar voice.

A young man in courier's clothes and a bike helmet stumbled back a step and held up a fragrant brown bag as a shield. "General Gao's!" he repeated. "Pork fried rice." He pointed to Max's door. "You're in 5A, right?"

"Of course." Thinking fast, Raine dug her wallet out of her purse. "How much do I owe you?"

She paid him, added a generous tip and waited until he was gone, until she was alone in the hallway.

Then she faced Max's door and took a deep breath. "Well, here goes nothing."

She wasn't giving up on her company.

According to Jeff, the FDA investigators had practically locked down Rainey Days while they pored over the computer and hard-copy files of the clinical trials. They were checking to see whether Thriller was safe for human use. They were also looking for evidence of criminal misconduct. Falsified evidence. Mysteriously "lost" toxicity reports.

Though she knew they would find no such thing, Raine didn't dare trust the system. Her childhood had taught her that much. Besides, the FDA was part of the government, and elections were on the horizon. If a competing company started throwing its financial weight around with influential candidates, she could be in deep trouble.

She needed her own investigation, damn it. She would've preferred to hire William Caine, but he'd claimed he was over-booked, that Max would have to help her.

Granted, he'd said that *after* he'd figured out who she was.

"Fine," she said under her breath. "We'll do it the hard way."

She unbuttoned her long coat, tugged on the hem of her camel-colored sweater and faced the door squarely, trying to look like the boss of a growing company.

Then she knocked. "Delivery."

She heard his footsteps on the hardwood floor she'd glimpsed just inside the door. When the steps paused but the locks didn't disengage, she held the bag up and stared at the fish-eye peephole. "You want your dinner? Let me in."

It felt like forever before she heard the locks turn. The door opened and Max glared out. His shirt was buttoned now, and he had thick socks on his feet and a knit cap pulled over his short dark hair. "I don't remember you being this bossy before."

"You didn't know me before," she said, telling herself that the flutter in her stomach was nothing more complicated than nerves.

She expected a snappy rejoinder, or maybe agreement.

Instead, she got an inscrutable stare.

When the silence grew long and uncomfortable, she cleared her throat. "I want to hire you to help me prove that Thriller didn't kill those women. I'm afraid the only way to do that is to figure out what *did* kill them. I can't do that by myself. I need an investigator. A good one. If—no *when* we succeed, it could be a huge boost to Vasek and Caine. I'll give you all the credit, whatever publicity you want. TV appearances, ads, you name it." She held out the paper bag. "Will you at least hear me out?"

He looked from the bag to her, and she

knew he wasn't weighing the food bribe. He was trying to decide whether the good of his company outweighed their history.

As the boss of her own start-up, Raine knew what the answer had to be. Practicality would win over emotion every time.

Otherwise, she wouldn't be here, would she?

Finally, he stepped back and muttered, "Come in."

The thrill of victory was dampened by the sly shift of heat when she walked past him, the shimmer of awkwardness at being inside his space.

The discomfort increased when she looked around. The apartment was large and airy, with carved moldings and neutrally painted walls. The hardwood floors were worn but well varnished, stretching from the tiles of an open kitchen nook, through the main living space, and narrowing into a hallway and glimpses of other rooms. She could see the small details of the hand carved woodwork on the trim and doors, mainly because that was almost the only thing *to* see. The apartment was bare, as though he'd just arrived and the moving vans hadn't caught up yet.

Yet downstairs, the label on his mailbox was yellow with age.

"Nice place," she said faintly, wanting to ask but knowing she didn't have the right.

The living-room furnishings consisted of a smallish plasma-screen TV bolted to one wall and a single faux-leather chair with a trash basket beside it. The TV sat in a square of darker paint, as though it had taken the place of a larger set.

Max cleared his throat and avoided her eyes. "My roommate moved out and took a bunch of stuff a few months back. I haven't had a chance to replace the things yet."

"I just figured your decorator was a minimalist," Raine said, trying for a joke when there was no laughter to be had. She held out his dinner. "Are you sharing?"

He snagged the bag. "Not on your life. Start talking."

When he went into the kitchen, she took another look around, wondering what had happened. Was the roommate thing true, or had his furniture been repossessed?

It struck her then that while Max didn't know anything about her, the same was equally true in reverse.

So why did it feel as if they'd known each other so very well?

He reappeared with a white carton in one hand and a fork in the other. He propped a hip on the corner of a granite countertop and dug in. "Clock's ticking."

She held out the file folder she'd assembled back at the office in New Bridge. "It's all in here—everything we've managed to pull together on the clinical trials and the four dead women. It's not much, which is why we need a professional. My people are scientists and marketers, not pharmaceutical investigators."

Then again, Max had been a scientist when she'd known him. What had changed?

"Is there anything besides optimism that makes you think your drug wasn't responsible for the deaths?" he asked, his tone making the question seem like a dig. "I mean, clinical trials usually contain what, a few thousand people? If there's a rare risk factor, it's entirely possible that your sample populations might not have contained an example. You might just have missed it."

Raine dug her fingernails into her palms, knowing the scenario he painted was one-hundred-percent possible. But that wasn't the explanation for the deaths. She knew it. She felt it.

Optimism? Perhaps. But right now it was her only hope.

"Our clinical trials were exhaustive," she said, knowing that didn't really answer his question. "We used computers to test out another million or so models. All negative. Besides, the dead women don't share any risk factors."

"None that you've found yet." He nodded at the file in her hands.

"Which is why I need your help," she said quietly, mustering as much dignity as she could. When his expression didn't change, didn't soften, she let out a small defeated sigh. "What will it take to get you onboard? Do you want me to apologize again? Double your hourly rate? Get down on my knees and beg?" She would do it if she had to, for the sake of the company she'd built from nothing. For the sake of her future. Her employees' futures.

A heavy weight settled on her shoulders, feeling like each of the dreams she let herself imagine late at night.

He stared at her for a long moment, giving nothing away. Then he gestured with his fork. "Leave your info. I'll have a look at it and talk to William. Call the office in the morning and set up a real appointment. I'll let you know then."

Instead of relief, Raine felt a new layer of tension settle. "Let me know what?"

"Whether we'll take the case or not." He sent her a hard look. "And if we do, it won't be because of Boston, apology or not."

A faint chill skittered across her skin, warning her that the agreeable Max Vasek she'd known before might not be the only side of him.

She'd known she would have to work to get past his initial resistance. Now, she reevaluated, and came up thinking that she might never get past it. She could only hope they'd manage to work together in a sort of armed truce.

She nodded slowly. "I understand." She turned toward the door, only then realizing that she could see her breath. The apartment was bitter cold. Another sign that Max's finances were in trouble?

She turned back and confessed, "I can't pay a retainer. That's why the others wouldn't take the case."

He shrugged, expression shuttered. "If we take the case, William and I will keep track of our hours and expenses, and you can pay us when it's over." Now his eyes focused on her. "Can I trust that you won't run away from the debt?"

She wasn't sure if the faint mockery in his tone was directed at her or himself, but she knew she wasn't going to find a better deal elsewhere. If Thriller went back on the market, it would take months—maybe longer—for sales to rebound, but they *would* rebound. Then she'd be solvent and able to pay. If Thriller wound up banned from the market…

Hell, she'd probably have to sell off the rest of the Rainey Days drug portfolio to settle her debts. She'd find the money one way or the other, except that one way, she'd be a success.

The other, a failure.

She swallowed hard, told herself this was what she'd come to New York to achieve, and nodded. "It's a deal."

He dug his fork into the carton and turned his back on her. "Then I guess I'll see you tomorrow."

His message was clear. He would consider working with her for both their benefits, but that didn't mean she was forgiven.

WHEN THE TAP OF HER HEELS receded in the hallway outside his apartment, Max dropped the carton of fried rice onto the counter and scrubbed both hands across his face.

Well. Raine Montgomery.

Damn it, he hadn't expected ever to see her again. Hadn't expected to want her if he did. He knew better. But that didn't change the fact that his head was jammed with the sight and scent of her, that her husky voice sounded in his ears the way it had before, tempting him, challenging him.

She's no different than Charlotte, he reminded himself. *A professional damsel in distress.*

Lucky for him, he knew better. He'd been vaccinated against DIDS.

Twice.

He grabbed the phone and punched in William's number, trying to believe his friend had a reason for giving out his home info.

The two men had known each other at Boston General, where the ex-FBI agent had worked for Hospitals for Humanity, a part-humanitarian, part-undercover investigative group with branches at hospitals across the U.S. When the men had found themselves needing a change at about the same time, they'd gone into business and Vasek and Caine Investigations was born.

It might die tonight, Max thought as the phone rang. When William answered, Max didn't bother with pleasantries. "Damn it. Why'd you send her over here?"

William didn't call him on the rudeness. "I figured that given your history with her, you'd want to know she was in trouble."

Max didn't bother asking how or what William knew about him and Raine. William had known pretty much everything that had gone on at Boston General. "Why, so I'd help her, or so I could gloat?"

"Whichever lets you get on with things," William answered pragmatically. "There's more to life than living alone in a five-room unfurnished apartment in the city."

"I like being alone. So sue me." Alone wasn't the same as lonely, Max told himself. And it was sure as hell better than being used. "And just because I don't date as often as you do—" make that ever "—doesn't mean it has anything to do with what did or didn't happen between me and Raine Montgomery back at BoGen."

"Then it was no big deal seeing her, you don't care that I gave her your address, and you're taking the case, right? This could be the break we've been looking for, you know."

"Only if we find something the FDA doesn't," Max cautioned. "And no, I haven't taken the case yet. I wanted to talk to you about it first, since I'll want you to be point man."

"No can do. I'm tied up through next week at the earliest with that malpractice thing, and I took on a new pro bono this morning. You're on your own."

Max gritted his teeth. "Don't try to fix my life for me, Caine."

"Wouldn't dream of it. You're doing such a good job on your own." William's voice dropped a notch and the flippancy vanished. "Look—we both know you've been marking time ever since Charlotte left. Maybe it's because of this woman, maybe it's something else, I don't know. Whatever it is, you can do better. You can *be* better."

Max winced because he'd heard nearly the same words from his father a few days earlier, during their bimonthly phone call.

According to his father, Max was closing in on forty fast. He should have a wife by now, a family. Sons. Daughters. Little ones to come home to and play with, and watch grow into not-so-little ones, like his nieces in the old neighborhood had done.

And maybe his pop had a point. But between college and grad school, the wife hadn't happened. The children hadn't happened. Over the past couple of years, he'd been wrapped up in starting and then growing the new company. Then there'd been Charlotte. For a while he'd thought he was all set. Then he'd been less sure. Then she'd been gone. And now…

What was his excuse now?

"Maybe you're right," he said slowly. "Maybe I do have something to work out where Raine is concerned." Maybe that was why he'd opened the door the second time, knowing even then that he would take the case.

Not to be near her, but to exorcize her.

Which led to another realization. He'd already decided to take the case. For the company. For himself.

"Fine. I'll do it."

He hung up the phone, then glanced around the bare apartment, which seemed so much emptier than it had an hour before. He picked up the folder Raine had left, which was prominently marked with her address, the Rainey Days office address and several phone numbers.

Logically, he knew he should review the data and make a few calls from the apartment, or maybe wait until the next day and work out of the Caine and Vasek office downtown. Instead, he cursed and headed for the bedroom, where there was a mattress on the floor, a few boxes full of clothes and a duffel he kept packed for emergencies.

Fifteen minutes later, he was on his way to the scene of the crime.

On his way to see *her*.

RAINE SPENT THE TWO-HOUR DRIVE from New York City to New Bridge, Connecticut, trying to convince herself that everything was going to be okay.

She failed.

She was too aware of the vehicles in her rearview mirror, too aware of being jumbled up at the idea of working with Max, being near Max.

"This is business," she said aloud as she passed the line into North New Bridge, the suburb where she'd rented a small house. "Strictly business. Nothing personal."

Then again, it had been business when Max had watched over her in Boston General. She'd been hospitalized partly because of the pregnancy and its complications, partly because a killer had stalked Max's boss at the lab. Max had appointed himself her de facto bodyguard for a time. It had been business, not personal, but she'd developed feelings for him just the same.

"I was pregnant. It was hormones. I even convinced myself I was in love with Erik for a while there." When the words echoed back at her, she turned up the radio to drown them out, to drown out the knowledge that while she'd quickly talked herself out of the infatuation with her boss at FalcoTechno, she hadn't been able to dismiss Max Vasek's memory so easily.

Now it was the man himself, not the memory, who haunted her thoughts as she pulled into the driveway beside her small white house.

The lights were off when she let herself in, prompting her to grumble about needing to reset the automatic timer. She was a few steps inside the door when she noticed that the burglar alarm was solid green rather than blinking red.

"What the—"

A dark blur swung through her peripheral vision and a savage blow caught her behind the ear, driving her against the wall. Panic spurted alongside pain as the darkness grew arms and legs, and a man's weight pinned her.

"Help!" she screamed. "Help me!"

Then blackness.

Chapter Three

It was close to midnight by the time Max turned down Raine's street in North New Bridge, Connecticut. It was too late to knock on her door, stupid even to be in her neighborhood, but he'd decided to do a drive-by. Familiarize himself with the area.

It was a nice enough neighborhood, middle-class residential with good sidewalks and signage. Max glanced from side to side as he rolled through a stop sign, looking for trouble, maybe, or insight into the woman who'd knocked on his door. She looked like Raine Montgomery, but she was different. She seemed harder than he remembered. Sharper.

Flashing lights appeared in his rearview mirror, wig-wagging blue and white.

"Oh, hell," Max muttered under his breath and shook his head. A ticket for a rolling stop was just about the last thing he needed right now.

He cursed and pulled over. Instead of stopping, the cop flipped on his siren and sped past, sending a jolt of adrenaline through Max's system.

Raine!

Gut tight, hoping it was a coincidence, Max hit the gas and peeled back onto the road. He gunned his truck around the next corner and slammed on the brakes when he saw two cruisers parked half on the snow-covered lawn of a small white two-story home. The house numbers matched the ones written on Raine's file folder.

And the windows glowed orange with fire.

Max didn't waste time cursing or asking questions. He slapped the transmission into park, leaped out of his truck and bolted across the snow-slicked lawn. As he hurdled a burlap-covered shrub, he heard the cops shout something behind him, but he ignored them.

Heat radiated from the walls of the burning house, warming the skin of his hands and face as he charged up the steps. The iron railing of the banister was flesh-hot to the touch. Smoke tainted the air, irritating his lungs with the promise of worse to come.

Max twisted the doorknob, barely registering the singe of hot metal. Unlocked.

He barreled through the door and skidded into a smoke-filled kitchen.

Heart thundering, he cupped his hands to his mouth and shouted, "Raine? Where are you? Raine!"

He thought he heard an answer over the rush of fire, which was eating its orange, greedy way from the kitchen table to the counter, where a roll of paper towels blazed.

He shouted again, "Raine?"

There was no answer. Maybe there never had been.

The ceiling bowed down with unnatural fluidity, as though the walls themselves were breathing. A door on the other side of the main room listed sideways in a surreal yawn of heat and smoke. Or was he the one swaying?

Gasping for breath, sweating inside his lined leather jacket, Max crouched low and looped the edge of his flannel shirt over his nose and mouth while he squinted against the smoke and tried to get his bearings.

There was a short hallway ahead of him, opening onto what looked like an open living room with stairs at the far end, presumably leading to an upstairs bedroom.

He crossed the living room, barely registering the soft furniture, visible in the strange orange light that radiated from the walls, from the floor, from all around him. He was surrounded by the awful, animal rushing roar of fire. The structure of the house had been smoldering when he'd arrived.

Now it was fully involved.

Blood racing with urgency even as his brain faded from lack of oxygen, Max stumbled past the couch.

His foot struck something soft and yielding. A body. *Raine!* He dropped to his knees, needing air, needing to believe she was okay. He said her name, but the words were ripped away as the fire spread into the living room and ate at the couch, counting down the seconds before it would be too late for them to get out safely.

"Raine?" He coughed against the burning claw of smoke in his lungs and pressed two fingers beneath her jaw. "Raine, damn it!"

He felt a pulse, but had no time for relief. A splintering crackle surrounded them. The floor beneath him heaved. The ceiling gave way near the stairwell and the whole structure tilted to one side. This time he was pretty sure it was the house moving, not him.

He got one arm around Raine's neck and the other behind her knees and lifted. She curled limply against his chest, feeling too light, as though the life had already been burned out of her. Her arms and legs dangled, and her eyes remained shut. Was she breathing? He couldn't tell.

"Come on, baby, breathe." The words were raspy with smoke, broken by coughs. He stood and staggered, then righted himself and headed for the door with one thought pounding in his brain.

He had to get them out of there.

Fire nipped at his heels, at his clothes, at his skin as he crossed the living room and kitchen, aiming for a door that seemed too far away. His feet burned and stuck as the rubber of his boots melted, and he felt the rivets of his jeans brand his skin.

Something crashed behind him, too close, and he broke into a coughing, shambling run as he cleared the door.

He made it down two of the steps before he slammed into a firefighter.

Time sped up, gained chaos, became sound and a burning chill as a flurry of suited men rushed him off the steps and out into the night air, which was refreshingly, painfully cold in his scorched lungs.

A firefighter grabbed his arm. "Is anyone else in the house?"

Max shook his head, "I don't think so." He had to shout over the crackle of flames, which was now joined by the hiss of water from a manned hose, and the sirens of an incoming fire truck.

"No husband? Kids?"

"No," Max repeated. Her career was her baby. Her family.

"This way, sir. Bring her over here." A pair of paramedics hustled him out to the street, where three ambulances were parked, part of an emergency response that seemed too large and fast for the situation.

Max paused, considering. The flames had been barely visible when he'd arrived on the cop's heels. "Who called in the alarm?" he asked, voice raspy with smoke.

The nearest paramedic, a tall woman with short, frizzy hair, shrugged. "Don't know. Ask the cops—they were the first response units. You're lucky it was so quick, though. Another few minutes…" She gestured to an unfolded gurney. "Anyway. You can put her down here."

But Max barely heard the order because he knew the paramedic was right. If the alarm hadn't been sounded…if he'd been a few minutes later…

He tightened his arms around Raine and felt a stir in response. He looked down just as her eyes opened and locked on him.

There was no change in her expression, no flicker of recognition or surprise or fear or any emotion beyond simple acceptance. She slipped her arms around his torso, reached up, pressed her cheek to his and said, "You came for me. Thank you."

He froze, peripherally aware of the firefighters' shouts and curses as they gained control of the blaze, along with the growing crowd of gawkers and the hiss of the angry fire. He noticed all those things, plus the sting of burns and the catch of smoke in his lungs and throat, but the sensory inputs seemed so much farther away than the woman in his arms, who filled up a space that had been empty for longer than he cared to admit, longer than his apartment had been bare.

He shifted, intending to push her away, but she moved and their bodies realigned until her lips were a breath away and her eyes were locked on his. He saw her lips shape his name, and before he knew he would do it, before he could stop himself, he closed the gap between them.

And then, almost exactly three years and

three months after the day she'd walked out on him, he kissed her for the first time.

FLAMES. FIRE. SEARING HEAT. Raine could have blamed it all on the burning building, but that would have been a lie. The heat wasn't coming from an external source; it was coming from inside her. From Max.

From the spark they kindled together.

Finally, she thought on a whisper of memory, as his mouth slanted across hers and his tongue demanded entry. She parted her lips and accepted him, tasted him and wanted more.

She remembered wishing for him as her attacker had knocked her unconscious. Then she'd come to and known whose arms held her. Whose heart beat beneath her ear. Who had come to her rescue.

Again.

Max. She fisted her hands in his flannel shirt and held on as a maelstrom built inside her, around her, swirls of heat and smoke and sensation roaring alongside the pounding beat of her heart. She felt his pulse drum beneath her fingertips, or maybe that was the race of her own heart; she wasn't sure anymore; she only knew that he was there with her, beside her, pressed against her. He had come for her when she'd needed him.

He'd come. He'd rescued her, and—

And she was doing it again, Raine realized on a sudden shock of cold reality. She was putting herself in the middle of a rescue fantasy and grabbing onto the first man to step into the role.

She broke the kiss and stared at Max, whose eyes were very close to hers and dark with passion. She said, "Put me down."

He lowered her to her feet and kept a hand on each arm until he was sure she was steady. Then they stood for a second, staring at each other, breathing heavily from the escape, from the kiss.

She saw the flames in his normally shielded expression, felt the answering surge in her blood and nearly reached for him.

But she didn't. She couldn't.

What the hell was she thinking? She'd

been attacked. Thriller hung in the balance. She had to be the boss here, not the victim.

Not a woman.

She drew a deep breath. "I shouldn't have done that. I'm sorry. It won't happen again."

A moment later, between one heartbeat and the next, his expression blanked. He muttered something unintelligible and gave her a long, measured look. Then gestured to the gurney and the waiting paramedics. "Let them check you out and get you to the hospital. You'll need to be treated for smoke inhalation, at the very least."

She batted his hand away and stood on her own two feet, doing her best not to wobble. "Don't boss me around, Vasek. I'm fine." She lifted her hand to the back of her head and winced when she found a large, tender bump. "Okay, a few bruises and a sore throat, but nothing I'm going to the hospital for. Where are the police? I saw the guy who grabbed me. I can give them a description of the bastard."

She fanned the flames of outward anger, but the realizations bounded through her head in a terrifying litany. She'd been attacked. In her own home. Her place had been torched with her in it. She should be dead.

She would have been, if it hadn't been for Max.

She didn't know what he'd done to get her out, but she knew she owed him a hell of a debt, so she touched his arm. "A man was waiting for me when I got home tonight. He knocked me out, then set the place on fire *several hours* later. Don't you see? This could be related to what's going on at Rainey Days. It could have something to do with the Thriller deaths."

His brows lowered and he seemed to grow bigger and more menacing, though she knew he hadn't moved a muscle. "Exactly," he said, voice low. "Which is why you should leave it to me."

She froze. "You're taking the case."

Maybe that should have been obvious. Otherwise, why would he be in Connecticut? But she needed to hear him say it, needed to know she had someone on her side.

"I'm taking the case." He held out a hand and she shook almost numbly, two businesspeople sealing a deal in the strangest of settings, standing in the darkness as firefighters slowly gained control of the inferno that had once been her house.

Then Max's lips twisted. "I had planned on mentioning professional detachment, and how it would be a good idea to keep our previous association separate from our business deal. But I'd say that horse has already left the barn."

Raine lifted her fingers to touch her mouth, which still hummed with his touch, his flavor. "I don't know—" She broke off and took a deep breath. "The kiss was my fault. It won't happen again."

She couldn't let it.

She'd had little security as a child, bouncing from one foster home to the next, so many different schools, so many different friends that it was easier not to bother. Longing for stability, she'd been too quick to grab on when Rory had wanted to take care of her. Rory, who'd barely been able to take care of himself.

No, Raine thought, this time she was going to succeed on her own. She would hire the help she needed to prove that Thriller was safe, that something—or some*one*—else had killed those four women. Max was the best man for the job, but so what? That didn't mean she needed to lean on him.

Didn't mean she needed him.

He looked at her for a long moment, but before he could say anything a thin, graying man approached from the driveway, where a wide stream of water ran beside her SUV and down to the street, looking oily and black in the darkness.

"Is this your car?" the stranger asked. He was dressed in street clothes, but a uniformed officer hovered at his side with the deference of a subordinate.

A detective, then, or maybe an arson investigator, Raine thought. Lord knows she'd need one of those.

She stepped forward and was aware of Max's steady presence close behind her when she said, "My car. My house." She clasped her hands together in front of her body to keep them from trembling. "I was inside. Max here got me out."

"I'm Detective Marcus." The gray-haired man indicated the officer at his side. "This is Officer Nichols. Why don't you walk us through what happened?"

After providing her full name and salient personal details, she described her return home and what she remembered of the attack, which wasn't much. She was able to give a general description of her attacker—white, medium height, brown hair and eyes—but though she could swear she'd seen him up close, the details eluded her. In the end, she had to shrug. "He was pretty average."

As she spoke, she was acutely conscious of Max's presence. She was too comforted by the warm solidity of his body, too aware of his every gesture and expression, and the silent hum of tension that ran between them.

When she finished, he took over the narrative, saying, "I got here just as the second cruiser arrived on scene. There wasn't much smoke, and I could just see the flames through the window, so the neighbors wouldn't have noticed the fire yet. I take it there was a hard-wired alarm system in place?"

That earned him a long look before the detective shook his head. "It was called in from the two-family across the street. Unit A." He glanced at Raine, and she didn't like what she saw in his eyes. "Are you planning a trip, Ms. Montgomery?"

"No, why?"

He gestured for them to follow. When they reached the driver's side door to her SUV, he indicated an envelope lying on the dashboard. "Looks like an e-ticket. Mind if I take a look?"

Baffled, Raine started to say *go ahead,* but Max stepped between her and the detective. "Not without a warrant. You want to tell us what this is about?"

The detective's eyes narrowed. "Who did you say you were again?"

"Maximilian Vasek of Vasek and Caine Investigations."

The detective shifted his weight so it was equally balanced on the balls of his feet. A fighting stance. "Is there something I should know, Mr. Vasek?"

I'm standing right here, Raine wanted to snap, but she didn't because this was part of why she'd hired Max. She needed someone who knew how to handle cops and suspicions. She didn't. Jeff and Tori didn't.

They'd needed an outsider. They'd needed Max.

Only now that she had him, Raine wasn't quite sure what to do with him.

"We're not hiding anything," Max said. "And we'll be happy to show you whatever you want as soon as you get back with that warrant. Until then, I'm taking Ms. Montgomery to a hotel while you search the scene for evidence pointing toward the man who tried to kill her."

After treating Max to another stare, the detective glanced beyond him to Raine. "Don't leave town."

"Of course not," she said between numb lips. "I have a business to run."

Or more accurately, a business to save before it was irretrievably crippled.

Raine pinched the bridge of her nose. What the hell was going on? Why had someone torched her house? Max's words echoed in her brain. *The man who tried to kill her. Kill her. Kill her...*

He touched her arm, nudging her toward the driver's side of the SUV. "Get in."

She did as he directed, then scooted over the center console to the passenger's seat when he climbed in nearly on top of her, crowding her with his big masculine body. "Hey," she protested, "I can drive. And what about your truck?"

"I'll get it later." He held out a hand without looking at her. "Keys?"

She dug the spare set from their hiding place in the passenger foot well and passed them over. Without another word, he started the engine and popped the transmission into Reverse.

Keeping one eye on Detective Marcus, who was making a slow circuit of the front of the smoldering building, Max backed the SUV down the driveway and out, navigating between the fire trucks and splashing through the stream of dirty water that carried pieces of her life like worthless flotsam.

Raine saw a single high-heeled slipper in the mess, one of a pair she'd bought to celebrate Thriller's acceptance by the FDA. Her eyes filmed with tears.

Rather than have Max see, she turned to stare out the window, at the faces of her neighbors, whose expressions ranged from horrified to fascinated as they watched the firefighters pick through the smoldering wreckage of the house.

She swallowed hard. "Where are we going?"

"Like I told the detective, a hotel. Got any preference?"

She directed him to the Guildford Inn, a mid-sized hotel she'd used once or twice when she'd needed someplace to put out-of-town scientists.

While they drove, she tried to pull herself together. It was okay. She could do this. *Just think of it as time to regroup,* she told herself. *Don't think about the house or the guy in the house. Just think about a shower.*

But when she got to the check-in counter and reached for her purse, she stalled because it wasn't there. Presumably, it had been destroyed in the fire, along with her credit cards. Her walking-around money. Her license.

Pretty much everything that identified her as Raine Montgomery and allowed her to function in the modern world.

"I've got it," Max's voice said behind her.

Her face heated when he slid his credit card across the counter. Feeling awkward, she wandered away and stared out a window at the night-quiet street.

Was the man out there, watching her? Or was he long gone, having gotten what he wanted?

What *had* he wanted? Why had he been in the house in the first place? She didn't keep any valuables there. Hell, she didn't *have* any valuables besides Thriller, and even that might be worth nothing if they didn't work fast.

"Come on." Max touched her arm. "We're all set."

They rode up to the fourth floor in silence. It felt strange to walk down a hotel corridor with a fresh key card and no luggage, and felt stranger still to have Max open the door for her. She turned to thank him, to ask what room he'd be in, but he followed close on her heels, crowding her into the room.

When she stepped back, he turned and shut the door, locked it and set the chain.

He glanced at her, eyes hard. "It won't keep you in, but I'll hear if you try to run."

Awkwardness morphed to confusion. "If I *what?*" Then she understood and anger burned away the weaker emotions. "Why the hell would I run?"

The corner of his mouth kicked up, but there was no humor in his expression. "That's what you do. You run."

Her blood ran cold even as her face flamed. "Not. This. Time."

Not ever again.

He reached into the heavy leather jacket he wore over his flannel shirt and pulled out a folded sheaf of papers. "Then what is this?"

Raine took the papers, which proved to be the e-ticket Detective Marcus had asked about, along with a boarding pass and itinerary. They were all in the name of Corraine Asherton, who was apparently traveling to Madrid that night.

There was no return flight.

"What was the plan?" Max asked, voice dangerously low. "Hire me to make it look like you were sticking it out, then fake your own death in a house fire?" He muttered a curse. "All that about not being able to afford a retainer was bull, wasn't it? You've probably already stashed the money overseas. No doubt you've—"

"Stop it!" she said sharply, anger and denial forming a hot, messy ball in her throat. "Stop saying that! I wasn't leaving. These aren't my tickets. I've never seen them before in my life!"

His eyes darkened and he deliberately took a single step away from her, as though stopping himself from doing something he'd regret, or maybe reminding himself not to. Voice sharp, he said, "When you left Boston General, your boss tried to pay me for the time I'd spent watching out for you. I wouldn't let him, because I figured it'd been my decision to stay, and because the danger turned out to have come from inside the hospital." He shrugged. "Maybe I felt responsible, maybe I wanted to hold on to the resentment. I don't know. But I do know that whether I volunteered or not, you used me. You hung on to me and begged me to tell you it would be okay. You implied there was something between us, something we should work on once you were out of the hospital. That was a lie, though, wasn't it? As soon as you got what you wanted, you took off."

Raine braced herself against the words, against the sting of accusation in his eyes, which seemed bigger than the situation warranted. But she'd known this was coming. She'd been prepared for it, as much as she could have prepared to deal with a mistake as big as this one. "I know this sounds bad, Max, but it wasn't about you. It was about me. I couldn't deal with being around people who knew I had miscarried. I felt like every time someone looked at me, they were thinking about my uterus, wondering how I'd ended up pregnant by a man I'd already divorced. It was..." She searched for the word and finally said, "It was invasive."

"So you ran," he said flatly.

"I escaped," she countered. "But I'm sorry for hurting you."

"You didn't hurt me. You made me feel like an idiot." He looked at her then, and there was no warmth in his eyes. "I won't let that happen again. I'm not going to let you put me on this case and then disappear."

A chill shimmered through her body. "What does that mean?"

He shucked off his jacket and tossed it on the bed nearest the door. "That means I'm going to stick with you for the duration, babe. Consider this an added bonus. You've just bought yourself a round-the-clock bodyguard."

Chapter Four

"Are you trying to punish her or protect her?" William asked the next morning, his voice tinny with a bad cell connection and background noise.

Max leaned up against the wall outside the hotel room, partly to give Raine privacy while she showered and dressed, partly to give himself a moment of breathing air that held no hint of her scent, no warm sense of the false intimacy created by sleeping in the same room with her once again. "Would it make me a bad person if I said it was a little bit of both?"

William chuckled. "No. It'd make you an honest one." Then his tone sobered. "Watch yourself, though, for both of our sakes. This is going to be a high-profile case—it's going to play out in the media as much as in the FDA and the courts. If things go wrong and you're on camera defending her…"

"I won't be on camera," Max said tightly. "And I won't be defending her unless I have evidence worth defending. So far, I don't." Hell, he didn't have much besides the reports of four dead women, a thin file of papers that said Thriller shouldn't be lethal, and a house fire that was either attempted murder or attempted escape, depending on whether he believed Raine or the weak-seeming evidence.

"Just be careful, okay?"

Though Max knew William wasn't just talking about the case anymore, he said, "Don't worry. I've got it under control."

But once he'd hung up, his optimism drained quickly. He had a bad feeling about the case. About Raine.

Was she in danger, or just dangerous?

The hotel-room door opened, framing her at the threshold. She was wearing the same clothes she'd been in when she'd knocked on his apartment door the previous day, but the expensive black pants were worn-looking, her camel-colored sweater was snagged and smeared with soot, her red wool jacket hung limply and the hat was long gone.

Without it, she looked less mysterious and more vulnerable, an impression that was only heightened by the dark smudges beneath her eyes, mute testimony to the awkward night they'd passed, together, yet not together at all.

She'd tossed and turned well past 3:00 a.m. He knew that for a fact because he'd been awake, restless in his own bed, listening to her breathe.

He gestured toward the elevators. "Are you ready to go?"

"Don't I look ready to go?" she snapped, then pressed her unpainted lips together in a thin line. "Sorry. Not your fault. I just…" She shrugged beneath the sad-looking wool coat. "I've got one outfit and an SUV to my name. The FDA has taken over my office and some bastard burned down my house and put plane tickets in my car to make *me* look like the villain here. Worse, everyone believes it."

By *everyone,* Max knew she meant him. But was it the truth or an act? Ever since she'd reappeared in his life, he'd been jarred by the differences between Raine today and the one he'd walled off in the back corner of his memory.

The Raine he'd remembered—when he'd thought of her at all—was soft and a little tragic, scared about being pregnant by her ex-husband, frightened of the clotting disorder that had landed her in the hospital, clingy when it came to her boss, who'd been one of the few constants in her life.

Back then, she'd reminded him of his nieces, Deena and Diana. The girls were only a few years younger than him, but in the way of complex multigenerational Czech families, he was technically their uncle rather than their cousin. He'd been responsible for nurturing them in the rough-ish Czech-dominated neighborhood north of Boston.

He'd protected the "Double Dees" growing up, just as he'd tried to protect a hurting, vulnerable Raine. But how could he protect this new Raine? Instead of cringing from the danger, she was stepping into it, chin out-thrust, ready to defend her territory.

Or was that the act? Was she really just biding her time, looking to cut and run as she had before?

Hell, he didn't know.

All he knew was that part of him wanted to hold her close and tell her he'd protect her, that he'd never let anything happen to her. But another, smarter part of him knew that was a bad idea. She hadn't come to him for personal reasons. It was business this time, more so than it had been before.

He'd do best to keep it that way. He should just pursue his investigation, get the name Vasek and Caine out in the marketplace as positively as he could and draw his paycheck.

Then walk away.

ONCE THEY LEFT THE HOTEL, Raine insisted they stop at the nearest mall, so she could buy a few changes of clothes and other necessities. The look Max shot her suggested he thought she was being frivolous and feminine, but he didn't get it. She was the boss. Her people relied on her to maintain a certain image. And besides, she could hardly hold her own against the FDA investigators wearing yesterday's smoke-smelling clothes.

"Give me ten minutes," she said once he'd parked near the department store entrance.

He raised one thick eyebrow. "I'm coming in."

"You don't need to. I'm perfectly— Oh. Right."

He was coming in to make sure she wasn't in danger. To make sure she didn't take off. Both. Neither. "Fine. I'll make it quick."

But she paused just inside the doors of the department store, overwhelmed by the number of little things she needed to live life as she knew it.

Makeup. Underwear. Nylons. Toiletries. Everything.

Think of it as a business trip, she told

herself. *Pretend the airline lost your luggage and you need enough to look professional for a few days.*

She couldn't think beyond the next few days. The future was too uncertain. Too dependent on things she couldn't control.

Like Max Vasek.

Hyperaware of his stern, watchful presence, she quickly grabbed an armload of clothes that should come close to fitting. She dumped her under things and a casual outfit—jeans, a sweater and sturdy boots—on the counter and kept hold of a pair of trim black pants, a burgundy silk shell and a fitted black blazer. She snagged a few staples from the hair and makeup counter, then ducked into the ladies' room, where she put herself together.

The clothes and makeup were a shield, a veneer of competence slapped over a shaky core. She forced her hands to stay steady when she applied a layer of gloss over her painted lips, and fought the tears back when they wanted to mist her vision.

She could do this. She could handle this.

She could handle *him* and the heat that touched her skin when she was near him. When she thought of him. She was going to have to handle it because she was on her own.

No leaning this time. She didn't want to be that passive wimp anymore.

And she didn't want a man who was attracted to victims.

Mask firmly in place, she emerged from the restroom and nodded to Max, who had leaned against a nearby support beam with feigned casualness. "I'm all set. You getting anything?"

He shook his head. "I have a bag packed—it's in my truck. We'll swing by your place, pick up my stuff, move the truck off the street, and maybe have a look around now that it's daylight."

The last thing Raine wanted to see was the burned-out wreck of her house. "Can you drop me at the office first?"

She thought his eyes softened, but that must have been wishful thinking because his tone was brisk when he said, "For both our sakes, I'm not letting you out of my sight. Sorry." Then he pulled out his wallet. "Here. For the clothes."

Their fingers brushed when she took the credit card, sending a fine current of electricity dancing up her arm. She tightened her lips and forced herself not to jerk away.

Max didn't acknowledge the flare of chemistry—if he'd even felt it. "Make it quick. The sooner we get started, the sooner we can figure out what happened to those women, and whether or not the fire was related."

Despite her resolution not to lean on him, and the awkward intimacy of paying for her new bra and panties with his credit card, Raine drew a measure of comfort from his words.

She had a professional on her side. And if anyone could figure out what had happened to those four women, it was Max Vasek.

He was too smart, too stubborn to fail once he'd decided on a goal.

It was a short ten-minute drive from the mall to her house—or rather, where her house used to be. Now, it was a pile of wet, blackened rubble that looked faintly slimy in the cold mid-morning sun.

Max glanced at her. "Can I trust you to stay in the car?"

Irritation surged over a faint churn of nausea. "I'm coming with you."

He scowled. "You don't have to."

"Yes, I do. I might remember something that could help." She opened the door and climbed out, then shivered when a sharp breeze pressed her wool coat around her and brought the smell of smoke.

She didn't remember much about the night before, but the odor brought a slap of fear and flame.

Max stepped to her side and gestured for her to cross the line of police tape prominently strung across the driveway. "Stay close. Detective Marcus will be annoyed enough when he finds out we've been here. I'd rather not mess up his scene."

"Do you think he left someone to watch the house?" Raine glanced around, but saw only empty cars parked on the streets. There didn't appear to be any curious faces peering from the windows of neighboring houses, but Raine narrowed her eyes when she saw a red-and-white sign on a door directly across the street. "For Rent, huh?"

Attention already focused on the burned-out shell of her house, Max answered, "That's right, you were a tenant. Hope you had renter's insurance."

"Not me. Over there." She gestured across the street. "Didn't the detective say the 911 call came from Unit A? There aren't any curtains in the windows."

Now she had his full attention. "It's vacant?"

"Looks like it. What if…heck, I don't know." She broke off, not even sure what sort of a theory she could build. "That doesn't make any sense. If he wanted to kill me, why call 911? And if he wanted me to live, why set the house on fire with me in it?"

As she glanced back at her ruined house, the basic unfairness of it all grabbed Raine by the throat. Only days earlier, she'd been on top of the world, anticipating Thriller's release and planning public appearances with a blend of nerves and excitement.

She'd been alone, yes, but she'd had everything under control and was moving in the right direction.

And now? Everything was a mess. Her life was spiraling out of control. She was powerless. Helpless. All the things she'd tried so hard not to be anymore.

"You coming or not?"

She looked up at the question and found Max halfway up the drive, waiting. "Sorry. I'm right behind you." She caught up with him, trying to step where he stepped so as not to tick off the detective any more than necessary. "What are you looking for?"

"I don't know exactly. I'll know it when I see it." He led the way around the back of the building, where the simple landscaping had taken a beating. The shrubs had been reduced to scorched stumps, and where the mulch hadn't burned away, it had run away from the house in red-tinged rivulets, borne by the hundreds of gallons of water that had been used to kill the blaze.

What was left of the house still radiated heat. Or maybe that was her imagination, she thought as she looked at the wreckage, at the blackened spikes of charred and splintered wood and the haphazard disarray of ruined appliances, ruined everything.

She swallowed hard and tried not to think about the fact that she'd been in the house. That she could have died.

Instead, she focused on the immediate problem. Finding evidence of an intruder, something that would prove she hadn't set the blaze herself to cover an escape. "What about those?" She gestured to a mess of footprints in the now-frozen slushy mud.

Max glanced over, then shook his head. "Probably the firefighters." He stopped and looked around, scowling. "The heat melted off most of the snow, and the water and the foot traffic destroyed anything that was left. Besides—" he touched his toe to a half burned book "—it's going to be damned difficult to separate out something your intruder left behind versus your stuff."

Raine tightened her coat around her torso, chilled by the sight of the book, which had been on her night table. "Then why are we here?"

"So I could get my bag out of the truck." But the look he sent her suggested that wasn't all.

She stiffened and balled her fists at her sides. "And so you could see me back at the scene, right? What was this, some sort of a test?"

He shrugged. "I told you to wait in the car."

Irritation spiked toward fury. "And if I had? Would that have meant I was guilty or not?" She lifted her fingers to the back of her head, where the raised bump had subsided, but the skin remained tender. "For the last time, I didn't set the fire, I wasn't flying anywhere using my foster mother's last name and I'm *not* giving up on Thriller!"

Max froze. "What did you say?"

"I'm not giving up on Thriller."

"Before that. The name on the plane ticket was your mother's name?"

"My foster mother," Raine corrected. "My father took off when my mother found out she was pregnant, and Social Services removed me when—" She broke off and blew out a breath. "Never mind. The Ashertons were my third foster family, but I lived with them the longest, until I graduated from high school." She swallowed hard, realizing what that meant. "Oh, hell."

"If you didn't buy that ticket, then somebody else did. Somebody who knows you that well." Max watched her carefully.

She could feel her heartbeat, hear it in her ears. "Nobody knows me that well. My childhood isn't the sort of thing that comes up in casual conversation, and I don't have many close friends." Make that zero close friends, though Max didn't need to hear about that.

"Somebody knows," he said grimly and turned back toward the SUV. "Come on. I'll grab my stuff and we can get out of here."

Raine resisted. "But we didn't find anything."

"Yes we did. The scene jogged your memory, and now we know about the name. We know the intruder must be someone with inside information or enough pull to run a very good background check on you."

Hope unfurled in her chest. "Then you believe me?"

He glanced back at her, expression flat. "I'm not sure what I believe. Let's just say that for now, I'm keeping an open mind."

"Oh." Raine tucked her hands in her pockets. "I guess—"

Her cell phone, one of her few personal possessions that had remained safe in the SUV, chimed, interrupting her. She pulled out the small unit, flipped it open and checked the caller ID before she said, "Hi, Jeff. How are things at the office?"

She'd phoned in first thing that morning, and everything had been status quo. But now the young man's tone was deadly sober when he said, "Are you on your way?"

Raine's blood chilled. "Why? What's wrong?"

"The FDA investigators want you here, pronto. They found something, but they won't tell me what." There was a pause before Jeff said, "And there's more. There's a cop here named Marcus. I don't think he's with the FDA. Is there something you want to tell me?"

Raine's fingers went numb on the phone, and the smell of stale smoke churned in her stomach. "We're on our way."

She battled sick nerves as Max drove them into New Bridge and parked in her numbered spot near the entrance of the office building that housed Rainey Days. She was tempted to babble, to give voice to the thoughts that swirled around in her head.

But she wasn't sure whose side Max was on yet—hell, she didn't think he knew, either. So she clamped her lips together and twisted her fingers against each other, straining with the need to reach the office, yet not wanting to be there at all.

Until she actually heard the FDA reps *say full recall of everything, even the samples,* and *Thriller is banned from the market,* the worst hadn't happened. Not yet, anyway.

THOUGH HE STILL WASN'T SURE if the danger came from an outside source or the woman walking beside him, Max kept his senses alert as he pushed through the doors to her world.

Based on the whimsical company name and his past experiences with Raine, he'd expected something smart and creative, but with a thrown-together feeling. He'd figured she would go for something temporary. A cardboard cutout office she could pick up and move on a moment's notice.

Instead, he walked into a slick lobby of marble and chrome, with warm hardwood floors and an inviting reception desk. A circular metal staircase off to the right ascended to a second level, where offices opened onto a New Orleans-style balcony that ran the circumference of a two-story open space. A hanging mobile of a complex molecule—maybe Thriller itself?—was suspended from the ceiling, moving lazily in an unseen current of air.

The layout was attractive and functional. Modern. Well thought-out. Permanent feeling.

Not at all what he'd expected.

A low-grade hum of activity permeated the space, but many of the offices were dark. Loose knots of workers wearing business casual were clustered in the lobby, while men and women in more formal attire—suits and dark colors—carried boxed files or hunched over computers.

The scene could have been entitled *The Invasion of the FDA Investigators*. Max had seen it before, several times in the course of his and William's work.

It had almost always ended with bad news for the drug company. Surprisingly, the thought sent a stab of remorse through Max.

He glanced at Raine as they passed through the lobby and headed for the stairs. She greeted people by name, briskly but warmly, exuding a sense of purpose and control. She stopped for a brief conversation with a tech type and accepted a computer disk with a nod of thanks. She tucked the disk in the pocket of her blazer and kept walking, her businesslike strides exuding confidence.

The panicked, vulnerable-looking woman who'd fidgeted on the drive over had been replaced by a boss. A leader.

Someone who didn't need anyone.

She's playing you, a small voice said deep inside Max. *Using you. The moment you've bought her some breathing room from the arson investigation and the FDA's case, she'll be gone somewhere else, living under another name and laughing at you, calling you a sucker.*

Just like Charlotte.

Cursing under his breath, not sure where to draw the line between paranoia and healthy caution, he followed Raine up the spiral staircase to the second floor. By the time they entered a wide room that had glass walls overlooking the central atrium and Raine's name painted on the door, he had forced himself into investigator mode and told himself to damn well stay there.

This wasn't about the woman. It was about the drug. About the deaths. Maybe about the fire.

He'd do well to remember that.

In Raine's office, three men were already seated opposite the main desk, in chairs that were an odd mix of expensive leather and cheaper chrome and upholstery.

Max nodded to Detective Marcus, who dipped his chin in response. Raine gestured toward a sandy-haired young man, who was in his mid-twenties at the top end and had tired circles beneath his blue eyes. "Max, this is Jeff Wells, my hot-shot second in command. We both know Detective Marcus. And this is…?"

The third man—silver buzz-cut hair, wearing a suit and a bearing that put him somewhere between lab rat and military—said, "I'm Senior FDA Investigator Robert Bryce." He didn't offer his hand to shake.

Max's suspicions quivered. Like most federal agencies, the FDA wasn't known for its lightning-fast response times. It was highly unusual for a senior investigator to be on-site so quickly—hell it was unusual for the FDA to be on-site at all, the day after official word broke of four drug-related deaths.

Either a powerful figure was pushing buttons higher up or there was more to this than Raine had let on.

Max glanced over at her, but she avoided

his eyes and took her place behind the polished desk.

Another conference-room chair sat in the corner, but Max chose to lean against the back wall. He hiked one hip up to rest on a series of built-in bookshelves containing the sort of texts and business reports he'd expect to find in the office of the head of a start-up drug acquisition company, but for some reason hadn't expected to find in Raine's office.

The position provided him with an overview of the scene while giving him a little distance from Raine.

You're immune, he told himself. *You know what she's like.*

Unfortunately, his libido didn't much seem to care. Just as she'd been three years earlier, she was back in his head. Under his skin.

Business, Vasek. It's just business.

"What have you got for me?" she asked briskly, using a no-nonsense tone Max recognized from his dealings with her former boss, Erik Falco. Maybe she'd modeled her leadership style after that of the billionaire businessman. Maybe she still carried a torch for the guy, even though he'd been married for nearly three years.

And maybe it shouldn't matter worth a damn.

"I'd like your opinion on this data entry." Bryce reached for a thin folder perched on the corner of the desk, extracted a pair of stapled pages and slid them toward Raine.

She glanced at the first page, stiffened and flipped to the second before looking at the senior investigator, body completely still. Her voice was measured when she said, "I've never seen these before. They aren't from my database. Where'd they come from?"

Max knew her well enough to hear the shock beneath her words. But he didn't know her well enough to be sure it was genuine.

He leaned forward to read over her shoulder and stifled a curse when he saw the words *Toxicity Report* and *cardiac arrest.* According to the report, one of the women enrolled in the Thriller clinical trial had complained of having chest pains when she'd used the drug. Cardiac monitoring had shown that the woman had shown an irregular heartbeat when given Thriller. The arrhythmia had disappeared when she'd gone off the drug.

There was no evidence of cardiac toxicity during the clinical trials, Raine had said to him, light brown eyes reflecting absolute sincerity.

Anger flared through Max, threatening to grow to a conflagration. She hadn't lied to him about something that important.

Had she?

Chapter Five

Raine's heart rocketed in her chest and a thousand thoughts jammed her brain, each more vital than the last. She stared down at the toxicity report. The words blurred. "This is impossible!"

Agent Bryce didn't even blink. "This record and ten others like it were found in your clinical-trial database, Ms. Montgomery."

"No, you're wrong! No adverse effects were reported during the clinical trials. There weren't any toxicities in the database besides dry mouth and headaches." Aware that she was close to shouting, close to tears, Raine turned to Jeff. "Tell him how we went back through the databases right after we heard about the first death, just to make sure."

He nodded quickly. "I double checked myself. There weren't any cardiac toxicities in the database."

Bryce's expression flattened. "That's because they were deleted on Ms. Montgomery's authorization. You're looking at a data ghost my people pulled off the server."

Raine surged to her feet. "That's a lie!" She felt Max move up behind her. She shrugged him off when he touched her shoulder, but she took the hint. Vibrating with indignation, she sank back to her seat and hissed, "I've never seen those reports before in my life. If I had, I would have backed off on the clinical trials while we investigated the toxicities. There's no way I would've sent Thriller to market without checking into something that big."

Bryce made a noncommittal noise. "Yet your pass code was used to delete the records." He glanced over at Detective Marcus, then back to Raine. "You stood to make a ton of money in the first few weeks your drug was on the market. Maybe you figured you'd get away with it for a few days or weeks, even a month before the cardiac toxicities started popping up. When the death reorts started coming in, you figured you could grab the money and run."

Raine felt a scream building in her throat, in her soul. She stood again, this time with deliberate slowness. She pressed her palms to the surface of her desk and leaned forward to glare at Bryce. "I never—" she paused "—*ever* deleted a toxicity report. I didn't call 911 from the neighbor's vacant apartment, then set my own house on fire and accidentally knock myself unconscious in the burning building. I didn't buy the damn plane ticket, and this *isn't* all part of some big plan on my part."

This time she quieted when Max touched her shoulder. His voice was deep when he said, "I don't know about you three, but it looks to me as though someone is setting Ms. Montgomery up for a very long fall."

A shimmer of surprised relief washed

through Raine at his support. But before she could respond, Detective Marcus challenged, "Based on what evidence?"

Max's fingers tightened on Raine's shoulder, holding her quiet as he said, "For one, your hypothesis has a big hole in it. This isn't a cash business. The invoices from the initial drug purchases won't come due for thirty days at the earliest, and it'll take sales a while to peak. There won't be any money in the first few weeks for her to run with."

"Profits from licensing agreements, then, or presales," Bryce insisted. He narrowed his eyes. "I'll be following the money trail, you can bet on that."

Raine matched his glare, drawing strength from the man behind her. "Be my guest, but make it quick because you won't find a damn thing, and while you're doing that, the real arsonist is going to be out there, doing…" She trailed off, not liking the options.

Max overrode her. "More importantly, if this is a setup, then we've got a murderer out there."

She glanced up at him. "Murderer? What do you mean... Oh." She swallowed hard, her stomach free-falling at the re-alization. "Oh, God. You think someone killed those four women to make it look like Thriller has a problem?"

Max said, "It's a possibility that Vasek and Caine will be investigating as our top priority."

Bryce shrugged. "Suit yourself. I've already got my suspect and the electronic evidence to back me up." He tapped the thin folder. "These files were deleted using Ms. Montgomery's pass code. There isn't any access to the system outside of this building, and I bet you've got spyware on your machines, so it should be easy enough to figure out when and where the changes were made. I'll bet—"

"Wait." Raine held up a hand. Her palms were clammy, and the sore spot on her head echoed the beat of her pounding heart. "You're wrong. There *is* outside access. I had the techs build me a back door I could use from the PC at my house."

It had meant connecting the system to

outside communication lines, but at the time, the company had been so small it had seemed like a minimal security risk.

Now that risk loomed large and foolish. Maybe even suspicious.

Silence ticked in the room for a long moment. Max let go of her shoulder, leaving a cool patch on her skin where his body heat had warmed her. He moved around the desk and leaned back against the far side, so he faced the three men while Raine stared at his back.

But there was no mistaking the dark musing in his voice when he said, "Which would explain the attack on Raine, and why the earlier scans didn't find the data ghosts. The guy in her house was using the computer to input them."

Her head spun as the scenario made an awful sort of sense. "But that means—"

Max shot her a look over his shoulder, one that clearly warned her to shut up. Then he returned his attention to the men and said, "That means that Agent Bryce and Detective Marcus have some work to do."

Bryce stood, a scowl etched on his face. He fixed Max with a glare. "I'll be watching you two." He transferred his attention to Raine. "And don't leave town."

"Right. Stay put. Got it." Raine pressed her palms against the desk, holding herself steady. "I'll be here when you figure out who is trying to ruin my life, and why."

Her voice broke on the last word, evidence of the rage, the humiliation and the damned dumb confusion rocketing through her.

Who was doing this?

Why?

Bryce stalked out of the office, followed by Detective Marcus, who nodded briefly at Max as though acknowledging an adversary, or maybe a kindred spirit.

Jeff stayed behind. "Raine, are you going to be okay?"

Knowing he was asking about more than her health, or even her safety, she nodded. "Max is on our side." She hoped. "I'll be fine. If the FDA goons will let you into the system, have the techs work on those faked toxicity reports. I want to know when they were entered and when they were deleted. And from where."

The techs who'd built her the back door should be able to identify its use, but would that be enough? It would prove that the entries had been made from her house, but it wouldn't prove that she hadn't been the one to delete them.

She pinched the bridge of her nose and wished for an aspirin. A vacation. A friend.

At the thought, she glanced at Max, who had retreated to his spot by the bookcase. "Thanks for backing me up just now."

His expression flattened. "Don't make me regret it." He pushed away from the wall and stalked across the office.

He was at the door before she found her voice to say "Wait! I thought you believed I wasn't responsible? Or was that just an act for Bryce and Detective Marcus?"

He turned back. "I haven't decided what I believe yet. I just hope to hell you don't make a fool of me again."

And then he was gone, the glass door swinging shut in his wake.

Leaving her alone.

MAX DIDN'T GO FAR. Down in the office lobby—where he could watch both the front and rear exits, just in case—he paused by the front desk, where a pretty dark-haired woman manned the phones. He overheard the tail end of her conversation.

"Of course you're concerned, Barbara, but there's no evidence of a longer-lasting concern. You used your sample packet and you feel fine, right?" The receptionist's expression softened a hint and she chuckled. "I see. That definitely counts as fine, and then some. So hold onto the rest of the pills for now, and we'll let you know when you're cleared to use them again, okay? Great. Bye, now."

When she disconnected, all trace of humor fled from her face, leaving her eyes dark and worried when she looked over at Max. "How's she doing?"

"I take it I don't have to introduce myself?"

"Raine told me you're working on the case. I'm her assistant, Tori Campbell." The woman offered her hand, but kept her body language closed, making Max wonder exactly what Raine had said about him.

He took her hand, noting a mostly concealed flinch that told him far too much. "Call me Max." He nodded to the row of lights on the telephone, some lit, some blinking. "You taking all the calls?"

"No, we're using a service to handle the majority. There were a few I wanted to handle personally, though." She glanced away.

People she knew, Max surmised. People she'd wanted to make sure were still alive.

Tori Campbell didn't trust her own product.

Interesting.

"Did you know any of the women who died?" Max deliberately turned his back on the receptionist and leaned against the desk, so they were both facing out into the lobby, where the FDA investigators were loading fat files into sturdy cardboard boxes.

"No," she answered, "none of us did. It seems so…random. Those poor women and their poor families. I talked to the first husband on the phone when it all started, before the lawyers and the FDA got involved. His name is James Summerton. He sounded awful. Hurt. Confused. Angry." She paused. "I can't get his voice out of my head."

Her words resonated inside Max, where something clicked. He stiffened as he realized there was yet another possibility that could explain the house fire.

Revenge.

What if Thriller really had killed the women? What if Raine really had deleted the data records? What if someone connected to the dead women had decided to take matters into his own hands?

The possibility didn't ring as false as Max would have liked. Stifling a growl, he pushed away from the reception desk and faced Tori. "Do you think the drug killed them?"

"Raine is a good person," she said quickly. "She wouldn't have gone forward with the sampling and the advertising if she'd thought there was any chance of Thriller being deadly." Then the secretary pursed her lips and looked both ways, making sure nobody could overhear her say, "There are a couple of others here that I'm not so sure about, though."

Max leaned closer. "Meaning?"

Her voice dropped so low he almost couldn't hear it. "Jeff Wells has been pretty chummy with the FDA people. And he's been hanging out with the computer techs. He never used to do that."

Max watched her eyes, trying to gauge whether this was real or a personal agenda. "You don't like Jeff?"

"I've never had a problem with him before, but ever since this thing started with Thriller, he's been…" She shrugged. "Weird, I guess. Then again, we're all under a ton of pressure right now. If Thriller goes under, it'll take Rainey Days with it."

He'd heard the same fear from hundreds of employees at dozens of companies since he and William had gone into business. Now, though, it resonated on a different level.

A personal one.

Max scowled and shifted away from Raine's secretary. How could he trust Raine so little, yet still want to help her?

"I don't know," Raine's voice said unexpectedly from right behind him. "I've been wondering the same thing."

Max jolted and turned toward her, halfway thinking he'd asked his question aloud. But her eyes were focused beyond him as she crossed the office lobby with her cell phone pressed to her ear and her long red coat draped over her arm, as though she were going somewhere.

He shifted to block her path, interrupting. "You've been wondering what?"

She focused on him and her eyes changed, so slightly that he might not have noticed if he hadn't been watching for it. She clicked the phone shut and said, "Computer stuff. Jeff and two of the techs are in my office trying to figure out when those data ghosts were inputted. Maybe—"

A ripping, rending explosion cut off her words and a fireball erupted from the second floor, blowing away a chunk of the balcony. The heavy construction crashed to the first floor, narrowly missing a section of office cubicles.

Max shouted as an invisible concussion wall slammed him to the ground.

He instinctively grabbed Raine on the way down, tangling their bodies together so he took the brunt of the fall. Debris stung his back and shoulders.

The roar of sound and fury escalated to painful levels, seeming to go on for far too long. Cursing, Max rolled them behind Tori's desk, where they were partway shielded by the solid wood kiosk.

An unearthly groan rose above the fading roar of explosion. Aware of Raine beneath him, of Tori and two FDA drones huddled in the lee of the reception desk, Max risked a look just in time to see the giant hanging mobile snap from its cable. The huge model crashed to the ground and splintered into brightly colored shrapnel.

The noise faded slowly.

And the screams and shouts began.

Almost as an afterthought, fire alarms

shrilled to life. The fire suppression system activated with a thump and water sprayed, not from the overhead sprinklers, but from ruptured pipes along the walls and in the ceiling far above them, pouring down in haphazard sluices that added nothing but wet and noise.

"Everybody out!" Max shoved Raine toward the main office door and gestured for Tori and the FDA agents to follow. "Outside, into the parking lot. The whole building could come down around our ears!"

As he said that, the other half of the balcony let go partway, sagging directly over a handful of cubicles, where workers cowered beneath their desks.

"I'm staying!" Raine yanked away from him, face gray with shock and drywall dust. "These are my people! That was my *office!*"

"These are your people, too." He gestured to the small knot huddled behind the desk. "Get them out and call 911." He got them up and moving out the door before he turned back to the destruction.

Without the balcony, the entire second

floor was inaccessible, with office doors opening onto thin air. A giant hole gaped where Raine's office had been moments earlier.

Jeff and two of the techs are in my office trying to figure out when those data ghosts were inputted, she'd said, which gave Max four immediate suspects for the bombing— Jeff, the techs and Raine herself.

It couldn't have been Raine, he thought instantly, sure of her innocence for the first time, though he couldn't have said why.

Even as the possibilities snapped into his mind, he was moving—not toward the door, but deeper into the office, toward the cubicles. He could hear moans and shouts and prayers, a litany of human misery. "Come on!" he shouted, coughing against the plaster dust and acrid smoke. "Everyone out!"

As though they'd been waiting for someone to tell them it was clear, a half-dozen people bolted for the exit, skidding on the wreckage. Farther into the cube farm, where a chunk of balcony had landed, he heard voices shouting for help.

"What can I do?" Raine's voice asked from behind him.

Max spun. Her face was bloodless, her eyes huge in her face, sending a stab of something hot and ugly through his chest. "I told you to go outside and call this in."

She gestured behind her, where Tori and the two FDA agents stood, looking grim but determined. "They're on their way. Until then, we're helping."

Max wanted to argue, but she was right, damn it.

He glanced up at the raw edge of wall where the balcony had been and saw faces peering out of three different office doors, heard more calls for help. Nothing was shifting, and it seemed like the building was structurally okay.

For now.

"Take that side—" Max's voice broke and he coughed out a lungful of dust and grit before saying, "If they're mobile, get them out. If they're too wounded to move, mark their positions for the professionals. Got it?"

The others nodded and headed deeper

into the office, which had gone from tasteful to rubble in the blink of an eye.

Raine brushed his shoulder in passing. "Thank you."

He wasn't sure if she was thanking him for pushing her to safety during the first fury of the blast or for not arguing harder against her help. Either way, her touch poked at a raw, sore spot inside. He bared his teeth. "Don't thank me yet. You were one of the last people in that office."

She glanced up at the gaping hole where her space had been. "I know. I could've been—" She broke off and looked at him, eyes narrowing. "What are you suggesting, that I blew up my own office with Jeff and two computer techs in it?" Her voice rose as she spoke, until it cracked with airborne dust and stress, or maybe with fear. "Listen, you—" She pressed her lips together and tears made her eyes shimmer with sincerity, or maybe pure rage. "I didn't. I wouldn't have." She looked down at the shattered mobile. A tear broke free and tracked through the dust on her cheek. "Never."

It clicked in his brain then. The reason he knew she was telling the truth.

Only it wasn't pretty.

"I believe you," he said, damning the ache in his chest when she looked up and hope flickered in her eyes. "I believe that you didn't set the bomb. And do you want to know why?"

Another tear joined the first. "Why?"

The ache snapped in his chest and died, and he heard himself say the words as though they'd come from someone else, someone standing far away.

"Because if you couldn't bring yourself to have an abortion when you so clearly didn't want your ex-husband's child, I can't see you killing people just to get what you want." He straightened as he rose to tower over her. He hated that it gave him some measure of pleasure to say, "Even you aren't that selfish, Raine."

Then he turned and walked away, feeling like hell.

Chapter Six

Raine told herself the wetness on her cheeks was spray from a broken pipe nearby as she tugged on a pile of debris, trying to free part of a cube wall without sending the rest crashing down on a middle-aged guy wearing the dark suit of an FDA agent and the scared expression of a man who'd seen his own life nearly end.

"Careful," he said for the tenth time. "Careful there." He tugged at his leg, which was pinned beneath the lower edge of the wall.

"I've got it." Raine sniffed against more tears. Concentrate. She had to concentrate on what needed to be done right now.

There would be time for tears later. In private.

The wall gave suddenly, sending her staggering back, where she collided with an immovable male body.

She didn't need to turn to know instantly who it was. Her senses were attuned to Max, damn them.

Damn him.

"Leave it," he ordered with enough bite in his tone to have her bristling in return.

"I can do it." She turned her back on him, hoping he'd go away. Far away. The sting of his logic was too fresh for her to deal with. Too true to brush off.

She hadn't wanted Rory's child, hadn't wanted the responsibility of single motherhood. She'd even considered the alternative before deciding it wasn't the right choice for her, practicalities aside.

But what Max didn't know, or chose not to remember, was that in those last few days before her miscarriage, in the days he'd been watching over her, her growing child had gone from being "the pregnancy" in her mind to being "the baby." Her baby.

Damn him for not remembering that, and for using what had happened against her.

Now, he gripped her upper arms and urged her toward the doors, away from the destruction. "The professionals are here. Let them deal with it."

She saw firefighters and a group of paramedics followed by beefy men carrying power tools. Even as they descended upon the wreck of her life, the building shifted with an ominous groan.

"Out." Max sent her toward the door with an unceremonious shove. "Now."

She half hoped he would stay behind, giving her a few moments without his too judgmental presence. Instead he remained close as she exited the office and followed a stream of evacuees from other floors, down the winding stairwell to the parking lot.

It was daylight. Sunny. Pretty. The sky was blue and patches of snow were melting. It looked like any other day. How could things seem so normal out here when the situation was so incredibly not normal?

"Raine." Max touched her arm, voice

subdued. "I'm sorry for what I said up there. I was out of line."

"Yes, you were." She lifted her chin, refusing to let the hurt show.

"I apologize."

The honest regret in his eyes eased something deep inside her. She slanted him a look. "Does that mean you're back to thinking I planned all this on my own?"

He grimaced. "I'm not—"

"Ms. Montgomery," Detective Marcus interrupted, appearing at her side with Agent Bryce in tow. "I'd like to have a few words with you."

Max ranged himself at her shoulder. "Detective," he said. "You got here quickly."

"I was in the neighborhood," Marcus said, no hint of humor in his expression to acknowledge that he'd left the office no more than thirty minutes before it was destroyed. "I'd like you to come to the station."

"So I've graduated to being questioned at the station," Raine said, tears and smoke turning her voice husky. "That either means you believe I'm responsible for all this, or you think I'm a target."

"I don't think there's any question of that, Ms. Montgomery," the detective said, giving no hint which side of the fence he stood on. He gestured to a plain sedan. "If you'll come with me?"

Though it bordered on leaning, Raine glanced up at Max. He nodded slightly. "Go ahead. I'll follow in your car."

Swallowing tears of fear and humiliation, she climbed into the sedan and sat in the back like a criminal.

Alone.

WHEN MAX ENTERED the police station later that afternoon, he was armed with more questions than answers.

Or rather, the answers he had were ones he didn't like. Not one bit.

He followed the desk officer's directions up a short flight of stairs to a wide hallway. Closed doors marched in rows on either side, fake wood panels that made the off-gray paint on the walls look dingy.

At the end of the hall, Raine sat on a

stiff-looking wooden bench, looking gray herself, though not dingy. Her clothes were badly wrinkled and streaked with plaster dust, and her hair had mostly sagged from its habitual twist atop her head.

Max paused mid-stride as the sight of her reached inside him and grabbed at something. His heart, maybe, or even deeper than that. Damn her for being so beautiful, he thought. Damn him for being a sucker. He forced himself to keep walking when part of him wanted to head down the stairs and never look back. But that would be running away, and that was her routine, not his.

Never his.

"Have you been waiting long?" he asked, his voice coming out deeper than he'd intended.

She shook her head. "A few minutes. I was gathering my strength to call a cab."

He scowled and snapped, "No cabs. No going out alone. Not until we figure out who's after you, what they want and how we can stop them. Got it?"

He halfway expected her to leap up and

get in his face, reminding him she was the boss, she was in charge. Instead, a worried pinch developed at the corners of her eyes. "So you *do* believe I'm not the villain here. What do you know that I don't?"

He'd thought about shielding her from the information. Instead, he went with the blunt, naked truth. "Tori and Agent Bryce helped put together a head count of who should've been in the office. Everyone's been accounted for except Jeff and the two techs. But there were only two bodies in your office."

Someone hadn't been where he was supposed to be. Their bomber, perhaps?

She paled further, swallowed and nodded. It took a moment, but she met his eyes when she said, "I hope Jeff got out. Then again, part of me hopes he didn't."

"They don't know yet." Max thought of the charred remains and grimaced. "They're probably going to need DNA samples for comparison."

"Oh." Raine looked down at her hands. "God. Those poor men. And Jeff. He was practically a kid."

Feeling the ache of the day in his soul, Max squatted down so he was eye level with her, close enough to see the wariness in her expression. "It'll be okay," he said, knowing it probably wouldn't be. "We'll get through this." Almost without thinking, he took her hands and squeezed them when he felt the shocky cold of her skin. "I'm here for you."

Their eyes met on a singe of memory.

I'm here for you, he'd said back at Boston General, giving her reassurance when she'd needed it, when she'd had nobody on her side. She'd leaned on him when she'd needed him, and left when she hadn't.

A familiar pattern.

He pulled his hands away abruptly and stood. "Come on," he said gruffly, more mad at himself than her. "The SUV's outside."

"What about your truck?" She stood and the worried questions in her eyes asked about more than just the truck. *What's next? Where do we go from here?*

Trouble was he didn't know what came next, and he didn't like the feeling one bit. He needed more information. He needed help, damn it, but William was flat out, and they were still just a two-man shop.

Lucky for him, he had an ally on speed dial.

"I won't need the truck," he said, answering Raine's spoken question and ignoring the unspoken ones. "I'm sticking with you."

"Because I'm a suspect or a victim?"

He started to brush off the question, but her expression cracked, showing him the need beneath the veneer of strength. Relenting, he said, "You're not a suspect anymore. Not in my book, anyway. Like I said, you're no killer."

Instead of relief, her eyes darkened with something hotter and more complicated. "Which makes me a victim."

"A protectee," he countered. He jerked his head toward the exit. "Come on. We'll find another hotel, maybe get a pizza. There's someone I want you to meet."

THEY AVOIDED RETURNING to the Guildford Inn on the theory that a moving target was harder to hit.

The idea of someone—anyone—watching her put a hard knot in the pit of Raine's stomach. But in a weird way, she almost hoped there was someone working against her because that would give them a tangible goal. A target. If—no, *when* they found her adversary, the Thriller deaths would be explained.

She hoped.

Their room at the new hotel was nearly identical to the last—complete with two double beds done in a generic beige print, greenish carpet and innocuous wall art flanking a central mirror. This time, though, Max had rented two adjoining rooms. While Raine sat cross-legged on one bed, he unlocked the connecting door and propped it open, mute testimony that he still considered her a flight risk.

She supposed it was an improvement over sharing one room, at the very least.

When a knock sounded at the door, she unfolded from the bed and stood, stifling a groan at the pull of bruises and sore muscles. "Pizza's here."

Max waved her back from the door and

checked the peephole before unlatching the door. "Nope. It's Ike."

Before Raine could react to the cryptic statement, Max threw open the door and pulled a tall woman inside. "Hey, babe!"

"Hey, yourself!" The stranger grinned and stepped into Max's arms. Their embrace lasted longer than dictated by simple friendship.

Long enough to have an ugly ache settling in the pit of Raine's stomach.

The woman pushed away. "Let me look at you!" Her ten-second perusal gave Raine ample time for her own examination, and she wasn't sure she liked what she saw.

The stranger was thin and looked whipcord strong. Her angular features were set off by a short cap of jet-black hair, and three gemstones winked in one ear. Her clothes were tight and black, and her boots had three-inch heels.

It should've looked overdone and foolish, but it worked, damn it. She looked slick and dangerous, and when Max half turned toward Raine, it became obvious that he and the woman made a striking couple.

Worse, the easy way they moved together made it clear that they were—or had been—exactly that.

"This is Ike," Max said. "Short for Einstein. She's a freelance information specialist. She'll figure out who did what in your computer system, and when."

"Oh." *Oh, hell,* Raine thought. This was the "someone" he'd wanted her to meet.

She gave Ike a second look, hoping to mitigate her first impression now that she knew the woman was going to be part of the team.

Nope. Still didn't like her, for no more reason than she looked good and nearly reeked of the self-confidence Raine so woefully lacked.

The faint sneer on Ike's face suggested the instant dislike was mutual.

Falling back on false politeness, Raine crossed the room and held out her hand. "Pleased to meet you, Ike."

"Here, take this." The woman slung two straps across Raine's outstretched hand, nearly dropping her with the weight of a computer bag that had to be full of rocks. "And this." A duffel followed before Ike turned back to the hallway and dragged a final bag inside.

The luggage was black and expensive, like the woman herself.

"That's all of it." Ike shut and locked the door to the hallway and took a quick look around the room. She pointed toward the small desk in the corner, where Raine had piled her sad stash of toiletries. "I'll set up over here." She cleared the surface with a sweep of her arm, grabbed the rock-filled computer bag from Raine and swung it up as though it weighed nothing.

Within moments, she had assembled a computer station that looked like something out of a science-fiction movie. "Talk to me, Vasek. And talk fast, since you've only got me for forty-eight hours."

"Pizza's here," he said apparently unaware—or not caring—that Ike had just completely taken over Raine's space without a word.

Max dropped the pizzas on the bed

nearest the darkening window and gestured for the others to join him. "Let's eat while I bring you up to speed."

Feeling excluded, Raine sat at the head of the bed, leaning back against the headboard with her legs crossed, wishing she could shower and change.

All she had left were the jeans and shirt she'd picked up that morning, but she was sore and bedraggled. She felt especially grungy in comparison to Ike, who scooted the desk chair over to the side of the bed and smiled in silent victory when Max grabbed a second chair and arranged it next to hers rather than sharing the bed with Raine.

"I gave Ike the general rundown over the phone," he said. "Basically, we have five things to explain—the drug-related deaths, the fire, the airplane ticket, the database entries and the office bombing. I can think of three explanations that cover most or all of these events. One, the drug is a killer and someone is trying to cover up that fact in order to buy time." By *someone,* Raine knew he meant her. She stiffened but didn't bother to protest her innocence yet again—he either believed her or he didn't. There was nothing else she could say. After a moment, he continued, "Two, the drug is a killer and someone—likely a bereaved family member or loved one—is out to get revenge on Raine and her employees. But that doesn't explain the plane ticket or the database unless we stipulate that Raine knew Thriller use carries a risk, and was trying to cover it up."

"Or three," Raine snapped. "Someone is out to get me."

"Not necessarily." Ike reached for a slice of pizza. "Could be that they want your drug off the market and you're merely collateral damage."

Raine started to snarl a response, but checked herself because Ike was right, and at least her explanation didn't start with the words *the drug is a killer.*

"I think we can rule out the first two options," Max said. He shot Raine a look before he said, "While I'm willing to believe you might fudge some paperwork on behalf of career and company, and we both know you're capable of taking off when things get tough, I don't see you setting the fire or bombing your own office. It doesn't play."

Tired of defending herself, Raine said only, "Where does that leave us?"

"Trying to figure out what's the real target here—you or Thriller," Ike answered for Max. Ignoring the pizza, she balanced a small handheld computer in her palm and held the stylus poised. "So give us something to start with. Who has it in for you?"

Raine simply stared at her. "Who are you again, and how are you going to help?"

When Max drew breath to answer, Ike waved him quiet and said, "My official title is communications director of Boston General Hospital, but I dabble in providing information to outside clients, as well. I know a little bit about everything." She reached over and patted the mean-looking laptop, which purred like an expensive sports car. "You give me an hour and a name, I'll tell you things even their own families don't know about them."

Raine glanced at Max. "I wish you'd talked to me before hiring a consultant."

"You're my client, not my boss," he said, expression shuttered. "You want me to figure out what happened with those women and your drug? Stay out of my way and let me do my job—which involves you answering Ike's question."

Stung, Raine said, "I don't have any enemies."

Ike's lips curved. "Everyone has someone who doesn't like them. You got a family member who thinks you got the inheritance he deserved? Bitter ex-husband? Psycho ex-lover? A former co-worker? Fired employee? Think a little. You'd be surprised."

"I doubt it." At the uptick of one of Ike's carefully shaped eyebrows, Raine blew out a breath and said, "Fine. Give me a few seconds to think." As though she hadn't been thinking about it for days now, trying to figure out who might be after her. Two minutes later, she was no closer to having a suggestion. She didn't have many friends, but she didn't have many enemies, either. She didn't consider herself the sort to inspire strong emotions. Killing emotions.

She shrugged. "I haven't got any family. I never knew my father, my mother lost custody when I was very young, and I grew up in the system. I haven't kept in touch with any of the foster families I stayed with, and wouldn't say I made much of an impression either way. Same with college and work. I'm…" *Unremarkable, she wanted to say. Wishy-washy.* But wasn't that what she'd tried to combat these past few years? So instead she said, "I can't think of anyone who would want to hurt me."

"What about your ex-husband?" Max asked.

"Rory?" Raine paused to buy herself a moment. Then she shook her head. "I don't think so. Not because I have any great faith in his moral fiber, but because this is too elaborate for him. It would've required too much planning. Too much effort."

She pictured her ex-husband as she'd last seen him, the morning after the stupid bout of goodbye sex that had gotten her pregnant.

An aging musician she'd met waiting

tables, Rory had never made it as a rocker, never managed to be anything else. He wasn't a bad man, or an evil one. He'd tried to take care of her, tried to protect her from a world that had given her too few breaks. But he hadn't been able to manage his own life, never mind theirs.

If their split hadn't been amicable, it had been necessary once she'd grown up enough to realize that security without ambition wasn't security at all.

Max was watching her intently. "Your ex might have resented the fact that you would have been a huge financial success if Thriller sales took off."

"I still could be a success," she countered. "I *will* be. Thriller is safe. You'll see." When Max raised an eyebrow and Ike smirked slightly, Raine grimaced. "Rory would be more likely to complain to his buddies over beers rather than actually do anything about it. Besides—" she shrugged "—when the money starts rolling in, I fully expect Rory to sue me for alimony. That's his style."

And she'd probably give it to him, partly for old times' sake, partly out of guilt that she'd never intended to tell him about the pregnancy.

"Then who could be after you?" Max leaned forward, eyes intent on her. "Your old boss? You left Falco in the lurch when you took off. Think he'd want to get back at you?"

Raine shook her head. "Unlike some people, Erik forgave me without hesitation. He understood that sometimes it takes distance to put things in perspective. And no, before you ask, I can't think of any co-workers or former employees who might have it in for me, either. I told you, I don't have any enemies."

"What about Jeff?" Max asked.

Ike's eyes sharpened. "Who?"

"No," Raine said immediately. "It's not him." More accurately, she didn't want it to be him.

"Your receptionist seemed to think otherwise," Max countered. "Tori said he'd been hanging out with the FDA investigators and computer techs way more than he normally did."

And there had been two bodies recovered from her office, not three. Raine grimaced.

"Let Max and me decide who is and isn't a suspect," Ike ordered. "That's why you're paying us. What is his full name? Stats?"

Raine sighed, but didn't bother protesting anymore. "Jeffrey Wells. He graduated with degrees from both MIT and Harvard last year, with every honor imaginable. I wouldn't have been able to hire him, except he wanted a flexible schedule and had his heart set on a position at a start-up pharmaceutical company."

Ike paused in her note-taking. "Why was the schedule important?"

"He's got a younger brother with some medical problems. Jeff is—was?—putting Joey through school while they waited for a transplant." Raine recalled the picture Jeff kept on his office desk and found herself wondering who had talked to his family. What had they said? Was Jeff dead or alive? She swallowed hard. "I still can't believe—"

"I'll check him out," Ike interrupted. "Anyone else?" When Raine shook her head, Ike said, "Okay then, let's look at our final option—corporate sabotage. Who would benefit from keeping Thriller off the market?"

"At least three other companies have comparable drugs in development," Raine answered. "Pentium, TopCat and Pyramid. But the rumors say their versions aren't nearly as effective as Thriller, and the nearest is at least a year away from being brought to the open market. I'm not sure what they'd gain from trying to—" She broke off and swallowed, struck anew by the sheer scope of what they were talking about. "God, can you even imagine it? Whoever it is, they've gone to a ton of trouble. Product tampering to kill those women, breaking into my place to change the computer records, then setting it on fire. Blowing up the office…" She trailed off as nausea swam in her gut at the awfulness of the list. "Who would do something like this? Why?"

"That's what we need to figure out." Ike slid her chair back toward the computer.

"I'll start looking at those companies, along with Jeff Wells." She glanced at Max. "Anything else?"

"Get me the names and addresses of the dead women's next of kin," Max said. He stood, scooping up one of the two pizza boxes. "We'll need to conduct interviews and figure out what the women had in common. We need to identify the risk factor connecting them."

Irritation flared through Raine. "I'm telling you, *Thriller is safe!*"

He lifted one shoulder. "Whether they were killed by the drug or murder, there has to be a reason those particular women died. There's some connection there. It's up to me and Ike to find it."

Raine lifted her chin. "And what will I be doing?"

Ike snorted. "Staying the hell out of my way, hopefully."

"We'll talk about it tomorrow," Max said. Pizza box in hand, he backed toward the connecting door. "Both of you be ready to roll at 6:00 a.m. We're registered under a safe name, but I don't want to stay put any longer than necessary. Just in case."

Raine stood and stalked past him into the other room. "Can I have a word with you?" When he followed, she shut the door. "What in the hell is going on here?"

He didn't pretend to misunderstand. "I think it's better this way, don't you? Besides, with William busy on other cases, I need an info tech to do the computer stuff."

She narrowed her eyes. "I don't need a babysitter."

"Maybe I do." The energy between them shifted, gaining an unexpected edge.

"Oh." Heat flared, pooling hot and hard in her midsection as he leaned toward her, eyes intent. "I—"

"Sorry to interrupt, but I think you should see something," Ike's voice said from the doorway. Max and Raine froze, then stepped apart as Ike held up a computer disk in a jewel-toned case and raised an eyebrow in Raine's direction. "Care to explain this?"

The label read *Database Remote Access Software.*

Chapter Seven

"Where did you find that?" Raine demanded, with an edge in her tone that set off all of Max's warning buzzers.

"In the pocket of your blazer. You have anything else on you that we should know about?" Ike's voice carried a similar edge.

Instincts humming on a faint twist of betrayal, Max crossed the room, took the disk from Ike and scowled at Raine. "This is the disk the computer tech handed you when we walked into your office. Why would he give you the access software?"

Raine shook her head. "I don't know. He told me it was a backup copy of the clinical trial database. I didn't look to make sure. Maybe he just reused the case?"

"There's one way to find out." Ike plucked the disk from Max's fingers and retreated to the other room, where she clucked over her computer, talking to it like a trusted friend.

Max moved to follow. As he passed Raine, she snapped, "I'm not lying, damn it. What do I have to do to make you take me at my word?"

He stopped and looked down at her, noticing the purplish smudges beneath her eyes and damning himself for caring that she was exhausted and nearly at the end of her reserves. "To be honest, I'm not sure. But I know it's going to take more than you telling the easy truth a few times."

"Well, this is one of those times," Ike said from the other room. "She's right. It's the clinical trial database." Moments later, her voice climbed a notch. "Wait a minute. It's time-stamped this morning."

Max was at Ike's side in an instant, leaning over her shoulder so he could see the laptop screen. "As in, after the data ghosts were uploaded last night, but before the explosion kiboshed the entire system?"

"If we're going on the theory that Ms. Montgomery's home invader inputted the files, then yes." Ike nodded without looking at him. "And before you ask, yes, I might be able to find the ghosts and backtrack them to their source. Maybe." She frowned and tapped a few keys before glancing up at him. "What're my priorities?"

Max muttered under his breath, knowing he only had Ike's undivided attention for forty-eight hours. She'd gotten the time off from Boston General easily enough—the head administrator, Zachary Cage, had benefited from her information enough times that he was pretty lenient with her schedule. But she was booked for the weekend, starting Friday. Max would've used someone else, but she was the best.

And, he acknowledged, Ike was the antithesis of Raine. That might have had something to do with how hard he'd leaned on his old friend to drive down from Boston on short notice. He'd needed someone he trusted to buy him some space and remind him not to be an idiot.

Ike had been the originator of the term

DIDS. If anyone could keep him from falling prey to a damsel with an agenda, it would be her.

"Hey." Ike elbowed him. "Sometime today would be nice."

"Sorry. Get me the info on the next of kin first, then see what you can dig up on Jeff Wells and the three drug companies Raine mentioned. Leave the database stuff for last, because it could be a hell of a lot of work."

She nodded. "Will do, sexy pants."

Max snorted at the reminder of a particularly embarrassing lab incident, and shook his head. "I'll see you two first thing in the morning."

He headed through the connecting door, then stopped and turned back to Raine. "Promise me that you'll stay here with Ike until tomorrow."

Raine narrowed her eyes. "Where are you going?"

One of the things he'd liked most about her in Boston was the combination of quiet reserve and a razor-sharp mind. Now that the quiet reserve was all but gone, the quick wit was almost irritating. Or so Max tried to tell himself.

"You're not invited," he said. "Stay with Ike. I want your word."

Raine lifted her chin as though leading for a punch. Her brown eyes were worried and defiant at the same time as she nodded. "I'll stay here. I promise. But only if you tell me where you're going."

"To meet an informant. Don't wait up."

WHEN THE DOOR CLOSED BEHIND Max, the two women traded stares. Raine broke first, turning away and grabbing her shopping bag from that morning. "I'm going to take a shower and change."

"Do I need to check the rest of your pockets?"

"No," Raine said between gritted teeth. "What you see is what you get."

Ike gave her another long look, and sniffed, making it clear she didn't think much of what she was seeing.

Raine's temper spiked. "Look, if you've got a problem with me, just come out and say it, will you?" When that earned her nothing more than a raised eyebrow, she said, "Fine. I'll be in the shower."

But just as she was about to shut the bathroom door harder than necessary, Ike said, "I don't like what you did to Max."

Raine turned back, confused. "Just now?"

"No. Back in Boston." The other woman kept her attention on the computer screen, her fingers kept tapping on the keyboard, but her voice held the weight of condemnation when she said, "He's a good man. He deserved better. He *deserves* better."

Raine winced inwardly, but tried not to let the sting show. "What happened is between Max and me. It doesn't have anything to do with you."

"You mess with my friends, you mess with me." Ike glanced at Raine, the light from the laptop monitor glinting off the three stones in her ear. "And whether you meant to or not, you messed with him when you left. He did some stupid things afterward."

"Like what?"

"Like taking up with Charlotte. She was

pretty and needy, just like you. Only unlike you, she stuck around long enough to nearly bleed him dry before she took off with a moving van full of his stuff."

Raine thought of the empty apartment in Manhattan. This time, she couldn't hide the wince. "Oh, hell."

Ike sneered. "You'll have to do better than that."

But Raine shook her head. "No, I don't. What I can do is tell you that I'm not interested in him that way anymore." Or rather, she was determined not to be. "I don't want a man who puts women on pedestals and wants to keep them there."

That got Ike's full attention. "He told you about his DIDS?"

"His what?"

"Damsel In Distress Syndrome. That's what we called it back at Boston General. Max has a near pathological need to save women, and isn't attracted to normal, healthy females who don't need saving." Ike shrugged. "He was losing interest in Charlotte even before she took off. Once she didn't need him anymore, she just

wasn't that much fun for him anymore.
He needs to be needed."

Though Ike's words confirmed Raine's
instincts, they stung her a little with the
knowledge that she couldn't win. If Max
was attracted to her, that meant he still saw
her as a victim. If she were able to prove
her strength to him, he'd lose interest. She
was better off staying far away.

Too bad she couldn't convince her libido
of that. Her dreams. Hell, even her waking
fantasies had begun to star Max Vasek in
lurid hi-def color.

Trying to make a measure of peace with
her unwanted roommate, Raine said, "Look,
I didn't handle it well—I won't argue that.
But it doesn't make me responsible for
Max's choices after he left."

"You are in my book."

Raine stared down at her hands. "I knew
how I felt—confused and scared and
needing some time alone to figure it all
out. But I didn't know how he felt. How
could I? It's not like he came looking for
me after I left."

A small, sad part of her had hoped he

would, even as the larger part of her had known they were better off apart. She hadn't been good for herself for the half year following the miscarriage. She wouldn't have been good for him.

Ike's eyes glinted. "I tracked you down about a month later and gave him your address in New Bridge."

Raine froze, remembering the crummy apartment in a slightly less crummy neighborhood, where she'd hit rock bottom and started the climb back to functionality. "He saw me there?"

"I don't know." Ike returned her attention to the computer as though she'd made her point. "You should ask him yourself."

"I will," Raine said. *I shouldn't,* she thought. It was too late to go back there.

Wasn't it?

"I'm going to take that shower now," she said to nobody in particular, mind reeling. Max had known how to find her. Instead, he'd ended up with someone named Charlotte, who'd left him with an empty apartment.

And though Raine told herself that

Charlotte wasn't her fault, guilt beat at her as she undressed and climbed into the shower. Remorse drummed through her as the water sluiced away the grime of the day.

And a wish to go back and do things differently hammered inside her as the tears began to fall.

MAX WAITED ON THE CONNECTICUT Interstate 84 overpass, hoping Charlie would show, hoping this wasn't some sort of runaround.

It was odd that his informant wanted to meet so far from their normal places, but then again, Charlie was a strange guy. He pulled down a hefty six figures as an attorney in downtown Boston, yet he sold information on the side for a few hundred a pop, and made his clients visit out-of-the-way places and use dumb passwords.

"Weird-ass James Bond wannabe," Max muttered under his breath. "Couldn't have picked someplace warmer, could you?" He turned up his coat collar and shivered in the rising wind. Below him, the occasional car zipped by, going from white high beams to red taillights.

He'd been there twenty minutes and he had yet to see another car besides his own on the overpass road.

"I swear, Charlie, if you blow me off, I'll—"

"No need for threats, Vasek. I'm here." Charles Lavone appeared out of the shadows, wearing dark colors that blended into the night. His salt-and-pepper hair was hidden beneath a black skullcap, and he wore tight black gloves on his hands.

For a crazy moment, Max thought the nutty son of a gun had climbed up from the road below. Then the other man swung a leg over, and Max realized he'd ridden in on some sort of motorcycle—black of course, running without lights and so quiet the engine noise was lost beneath that of the passing cars.

"You're late." Max shoved his hands in his jacket pockets. On the right side, he felt the comforting weight of his old revolver, which he'd brought just in case.

"And why the hell'd we have to meet out here? It's bloody cold."

Charlie stepped closer and dropped his voice. "I wanted to keep this on the QT." He paused. "Besides, old retrievers catch young chicks."

Max sighed, but obliged with the countersign Charlie had given him earlier in the day. "And young chicks like old dogs." He didn't want to know what that said about the lawyer's love life. "What've you got for me?"

"How's the ex-girlfriend?"

The good news about Charlie was that he knew things, often things too deeply hidden for Ike to find with her borderline legal methods. That was also the bad news.

Charlie knew things.

Max looked out over the sparse traffic below. "Raine isn't my girlfriend. Never was, never will be. And there isn't a soul alive—except maybe my mother—who'd pay you money for that info."

"Your love life's that good, huh?" Charlie smirked. "Sorry to hear it."

"I'm waiting." Max held out a legal-sized

envelope. Inside rested ten crisp new fifties. "It better be good. I'm freezing my—"

"I promise," Charlie interrupted. "It's better than good." He leaned even closer and dropped his voice to a whisper. "What do you know about The Nine?"

Max nearly laughed aloud. In a normal voice, he said, "You're joking, right? Please tell me you're joking." When Charlie didn't respond, Max scowled, pretty sure he'd been had. He pulled the envelope back and dropped it close to his side. "The Nine is nothing but an urban legend."

"Some urban legends are based in fact."

"You're serious?" Max couldn't believe his ears. "You don't actually believe there's a powerful group working behind the scenes to control the entirety of worldwide scientific progress, do you? Come on, that's *Wizard of Oz* stuff, not real life."

"Life. Fiction." Charlie shrugged. "Both strange. I'm serious. The Nine are real."

Coming from anyone else, Max would've dismissed the foolishness at once. Coming from Charlie—who was weird but almost always accurate—the possibility tweaked his curiosity. "Based on what evidence? And why tell me here? Now?"

Charlie looked away. "I don't have anything concrete. That's why the group is a damn urban legend. Besides, it's not in my best interest to look too closely. But I think it might be in yours."

A sliver of ice formed in Max's gut. "You're telling me The Nine is involved in what's happening with Thriller and Raine Montgomery?"

That was utterly impossible. The Nine didn't exist. The group was an easy excuse, an inside joke among scientists.

When an important paper was rejected for no good reason, the authors often said it was The Nine at work. When that last big experiment—the one required to prove an important hypothesis once and for all—failed repeatedly, the lab techs would say it'd been sabotaged by The Nine. And when a promising grad student, who'd seemed well on his or her way to Nobel-level work, faded into obscurity or left the field, it was whispered that The Nine had gotten to them.

It was all fantasy, of course. A way for researchers to explain the inexplicable that was all too common in science.

The group wasn't real.

Was it?

Max thought for a moment, then tried to tell himself it was just a coincidence that the plot against Raine seemed too big, too complex for a single enemy to have organized.

Still… He took a breath. "Let's say for the sake of argument that I believed this crap. Why Raine?"

"I don't know." Charlie peered into the shadows, agitation building. "And I've already said too much. I've got to get out of here." He held out his hand for the money.

Max tightened his grip on the envelope. "Not a chance. You haven't given me jack except—"

Charlie lunged at him and grabbed the money. Max nearly went for his gun, but stopped himself when Charlie pressed a hard plastic object into his hand and whispered, "Take them down. They suppressed a drug that would've saved my wife, just because they owned a competing drug. I can't do it—I have to think of our children. But you can. You and William Caine. *Please*."

Breathing so fast he was nearly panting, Charlie pulled away from Max. He took two running steps, jumped aboard the idling motorbike, kicked it into gear and accelerated across the overpass.

A shot rang out from the opposite side of the road. Charlie shouted and swerved, and the bike hit the edge of the railing. The momentum carried it up and over, taking Charlie with it.

Seconds later, as he bolted for his truck, Max heard a squeal of brakes and the sound of an impact from below.

He heard a second shot, but either it missed or he wasn't the target, because there was no burn of impact. He couldn't see the shooter. It was so dark he couldn't see much of anything until he opened the truck door and the interior light popped on.

Three shots came in rapid fire. Two hit the door and one spiderwebbed the driver's side window, leaving little question that he was the target.

"Damn it!" Max scrambled inside and shut the door, cursing when the dome light took a few precious seconds to shut off. He'd left the keys in the ignition, and muttered to himself in the half second before the engine turned over and roared to life.

There was no use returning fire. It was dark on dark. He was the visible target. Better to get the hell out of there and live to fight another day.

Live to see what was on the disk Charlie had given him.

The disk someone was willing to kill for.

Max stomped on the gas, twisted the wheel and sent the SUV hurtling across the overpass, slaloming in a crazy path that would hopefully foil his attacker's aim.

Maybe there were more bullets, he didn't know. He passed the place where Charlie had gone over, and accelerated when he hit the on-ramp that dumped him onto I-84 headed south.

Heart pounding, he turned on his headlights. The road was clear, with traffic snarled behind him where Charlie's bike and body had landed.

He kept his eyes on the rearview mirror, but no car followed him down the ramp.

The speedometer edged toward eighty miles per hour. "Damn it, Charlie. What the hell did you get yourself into?"

What did I get you into?

And how would he get the rest of them out unscathed?

Chapter Eight

Raine dozed lightly in the hotel room, kept awake by the chatter of Ike's computer keyboard as the other woman typed a few lines, paused to stare at the screen, then typed again. Sometimes she talked to the machine, low crooning words interspersed with the occasional mild curse and the click of her cordless mouse.

She didn't talk to Raine, but that was just fine. Raine didn't want to talk to her, either. Their earlier conversation lay too heavy on her heart.

Though she wasn't responsible for Max's actions, she was responsible for her own. She'd been selfish when she'd left Boston, and she was starting to realize a simple apology wasn't sufficient. She'd done damage on her way out.

How could she fix it?

"Your friend Jeff has a heck of a checkered past," Ike announced unexpectedly.

Raine opened her eyes and found the other woman staring at her. "Are you talking to me or your computer this time?"

"Ha, ha. That line and five bucks'll get you a spot at the nearest comedy hour." But Ike's words lacked venom, as though she was content to call a truce after their earlier conversation. She turned back to the computer and said, "He did a little time in juvie for petty theft and what looks like racketeering, though they don't call it that when you're thirteen."

Raine levered herself up on the bed, surprised that the bedside clock read 4:00 a.m. Apparently she'd dozed longer than she'd thought. She yawned and rolled her neck to ease the kinks. "I thought juvie records were supposed to be sealed?"

"Please." Ike cracked her knuckles. "Piece of cake. He was nearly kicked out of both colleges three months before graduation on suspicion of cheating and hacking test scores, but the charges mysteriously disappeared right about the time you contacted him about working for Rainey Days."

A chill sneaked through Raine's lingering sleep warmth. "I didn't contact Jeff. He came looking for me. Said he was interested in Thriller, and he wanted to get in on the ground floor of a major breakthrough." She'd been flattered, and more than a little relieved to hand daily operations over to a genius with a hell of a head for business.

"Of course he did." Ike rolled her eyes. "And you know that sick brother of his? He's all better."

Raine hated where this was going. *Not Jeff,* she thought. *Please not Jeff.* "That's impossible. Joey needs a transplant, and he's got some sort of wonky HLA factor that's almost impossible to match."

"They matched it. The surgery was done in Maryland last month. Private benefactor."

"Oh." Oh, Jeff. Raine swallowed hard

against the betrayal, trying not to show how much it hurt. "Any idea who paid?"

That earned her a raised eyebrow. "Hmm. Quicker than you look, aren't you?" Ike pulled up two new windows on the computer screen, tapped a few keystrokes and frowned. "Nothing yet. It's buried pretty good, but I'll keep at it."

"Not as quick as you'd like us to believe, are you?" Raine snapped back.

"I'd be quicker if you told us everything you know."

"I have, damn it!" Raine's voice bounced off the walls, loud in the night-quiet hotel. "And what's your problem, you—"

"Get down!" Ike erupted from her chair and yanked a gun seemingly from nowhere. She crossed to the bed, grabbed a fistful of Raine's shirt and shoved her to the floor between the beds. She mouthed, "Stay down and shut up."

For a heart-pounding second, Raine thought the other woman was going to shoot her. Then she heard it.

The sound of a footstep outside their door. At four in the morning.

It might be Max, returning from his meeting.

But what if it wasn't?

Raine peered around the edge of the bed and watched as Ike positioned herself beside the door, weapon at the ready. She checked the peephole, contorting her body so it wasn't directly in the line of fire.

Then she cursed and holstered her weapon. "Vasek, you idiot." Muttering under her breath, she unlatched the security chain and bolt, and yanked open the door. "Next time, call first. I almost put a hole in you."

As Ike relocked the door behind him, Raine got a good look at Max's expression, which was dark and brooding, and lined with tension.

She stood. "What's wrong?"

He took a step toward her and lifted a hand, then let it fall to his side. "Grab your stuff and let's go. We've got to get out of here. They killed my informant."

Killed? Raine stood frozen for a second, unable to believe that this was happening. That it was still happening. She kept waiting for the violence to stop.

Instead, it seemed to be accelerating.

"Get your stuff or you're leaving without it," Max snapped as he passed her on his way to the adjoining room.

Broken from her paralysis, Raine loaded the shopping bag with her few items of clothing while Ike packed her computer with practiced efficiency.

Voice calm, as though she dealt with murder every day, Ike said, "Where are we headed?"

Max reappeared in the doorway, duffel slung over his shoulder. "You're going back to Boston, and you're going to pretend you were never here."

"Like hell I am. Try again, Vasek." Then Ike stopped, faint humor draining from her face. "You're serious."

"Deadly." He looked down at her and his expression softened a hint. "I know you're tough, Ike. I know you can take care of yourself. Do this for me, please. Just go home and forget you know me."

Ike reached up and touched his cheek. "Poor Max. Still trying to protect me, aren't you? It never worked before and it won't work this time. I'll go home, but I'm not off the case. Call me when you can, and I'll update you on the database and Jeff Wells." Ike jerked her head in Raine's direction. "That one can brief you on what I've found so far."

Max stood for a moment, staring down at her, indecision written on his face. Then he muttered a curse, reached into his pocket and produced a mini-disk. "Charlie gave me this just before they shot him. He said it'd help me get the guy who's masterminding this. Call me when you have something."

Then he leaned down and kissed Ike on the cheek before he turned and headed out the door without a backward glance.

Raine seethed with a jealousy she had no right to feel. When Ike passed her on the way to retrieve her computer bags, Raine said, "I'm sorry. I didn't realize earlier that you and Max were an item."

Ike snorted. "Max and I are friends. Equals." She shrugged. "I'd go there for fun, but I'm not his type. He only likes women he can save, and that's not me.

Never will be." She narrowed her eyes. "I'd tell you to stay away from him, but I can see that'd be a waste. You already proved you'll think about yourself before you think about him. So consider this instead—even if he wants you now, it's only because you're a damsel in distress. Once you don't need saving anymore, he'll lose interest. That's the way it works. That's the way it *always* works."

MAX WAITED IMPATIENTLY in the hallway. He'd thought the women were right behind him. Didn't they understand how much danger they were in?

Of course not, he thought. *You haven't told them everything.* But how could he explain Charlie's wild accusation when he wasn't sure he understood it—or believed it—himself?

The door opened and Ike joined him, eyes sober.

He frowned. "Where's Raine?"

"She's coming. A few of her things fell behind the desk." She touched his arm. "Don't try to save the world, Max. If there's a body, the cops will listen to you. Hell, they're already listening. And the FDA's involved. Take it to them. This isn't your fight."

But if he bought into Charlie's theory, if he bought into the whole legend of The Nine, then there was a very good chance at least one prominent member of the FDA hierarchy was involved. That would explain why the notoriously slow-moving agency had moved into Raine's office at nearly warp speed. And the cops… Max thought of Detective Marcus and how chummy he'd seemed with Agent Bryce.

There was a fine line between conspiracy and paranoia, but he was damned if he knew who to trust at this point. And with more theory than evidence, there was a good chance that Raine would remain the primary suspect in the Thriller deaths.

Hell, they might even find a way to pin Charlie's murder on her. Reluctantly, he dug into his duffel and pulled out a pair of cheap disposable phones, part of the emergency kit he and William had devised.

He handed one of the phones to Ike and

put the other in his jacket pocket. "Take this. It's programmed with my number, and vice versa. Use it to call me, not your regular phone. If you can't get me, leave a message on my machine at home."

She looked at him for a long moment. "You're serious, aren't you?"

"I'll explain later. Get me those data ghosts and see what the hell's on that disk Charlie gave me. Once you have, I'll tell you what I can."

"And until then?"

"Do you have the contact info on the victims' families?" When she dug out a piece of paper, he took it and stuffed it in his pocket alongside the phone. "Raine and I will go talk to them." It was both a necessary part of the investigation and a good excuse to travel, staying with the theory that it was harder to hit a moving target than a stationary one.

Ike's expression clouded. "You could leave her with me."

His lips twisted. "No, I can't."

She raised an eyebrow. When he didn't fill in the gap, she sighed. "I was afraid of that. Watch yourself, Vasek. Don't make the same mistake a *third* time, for God's sake."

"I won't," he said, though what he really meant was *I'm trying not to.*

"Just be careful," Ike said. She patted his cheek again—a gesture she knew darn well he hated—and headed down the corridor.

"You, too," he said under his breath as the hotel room door opened a final time and Raine stepped through, wearing her long red wool coat and a scared expression.

"Give me your bag." Cursing himself for having not thought of it sooner, he dumped the contents of her shopping bag into his duffel and zipped it shut. "We're going to need to move fast. I'll explain once we're on the road, okay?"

Face pale, she nodded. "Lead the way."

"That's my girl." He didn't mean the words as anything more than encouragement, but as she followed him down the hall, the platitude resonated too close for his comfort.

My girl.

They didn't talk as he led them down a flight of stairs and through a back exit that spit them out in a poorly lit alley on the opposite side from the parking garage.

When he paused before stepping through, Raine whispered, "We're leaving my SUV, aren't we?"

The words were more statement than question.

He reached back and gripped her shoulder briefly. "It'll be safe in the hotel garage for a few days." He hoped.

"It's not that." Her whisper was quiet and a little sad. "It's just that I don't have much left that's mine. The house is gone. The office is wrecked. Now the car..." She trailed off and then squared her shoulders beneath her long coat. "Never mind. I'm focusing on stupid stuff. Let's go."

Part of Max wanted to hug her, to hold her and tell her everything was going to be okay.

Self-preservation had him turning away. "Keep your eyes open and your voice down. You got another coat in that bag of yours?"

"No. The red wool is warm enough."

"It's also too recognizable." He glanced along the deserted alleyway. Both ends were open and doors led away at regular intervals. There was no sign of activity. They were safe enough for the moment. "Here." He shrugged out of his parka, unzipped the fuzzy brown lining and turned it inside out, so it looked like a ratty fake fur coat. "Dump yours and wear this. Let your hair down, too."

She complied, and within moments looked like a completely different person. Gone was the businesslike, boss-like Raine Montgomery of just a few days earlier. In her place stood a smaller-looking version in jeans and an inexpensive sweater, wearing hiking boots and a shapeless brown jacket that nearly swallowed her whole. With her hair down, she looked younger, more vulnerable, as though changing out of the suit had stripped her of her tough-gal veneer, leaving only the woman beneath.

In the orangey sodium lights reflected from the streets on either side, she looked like the Raine he'd first met. The one he'd fallen for, long before he'd known where her priorities lay. The one he'd thought of in the years since.

The one he wanted to hold now. Kiss now. Sink himself in, lose himself in until it didn't matter that they wanted different things, believed in different things.

But because now wasn't the time and Raine sure as hell wasn't the woman, Max busied himself with reversing his parka, taking it from hunter green to tan. He retrieved a battered Patriots cap from the pocket and pulled it low over his eyes.

When he was done, it wasn't nearly as dramatic a change, but it should be enough to confuse the men who'd killed Charlie, the men he feared might have followed him back to the hotel. Back to Raine.

It would *have* to be enough to fool them because he didn't have a better plan.

Without another word, he turned and gestured up the alley, toward the brighter gleam of the street beyond.

They'd gone three paces when a door banged behind them.

He heard a *pop,* then a *pzzzt* as something

whizzed past his ear. His body was already moving before his brain caught up with the noise.

Gunshot!

"Go! Run!" He shoved Raine away from the dark figure of a man, who stepped into the alley, raised his silenced weapon.

And fired again.

RAINE BOLTED FOR THE MAIN ROAD. She slipped on a patch of ice and nearly went down, but Max was there, grabbing her upper arm and dragging her along in his wake. "Don't look back!"

She stumbled at his side. "Why isn't he shooting?"

"Good question." He slowed and risked a look back. "Maybe because—oh, hell."

A dark limousine pulled up at the open end of the alley in front of them. The door opened and a second black-clad figure emerged and drew an identical silenced weapon.

"There!" Raine pointed across the alley, where a rusted door was partially obscured by a Dumpster.

Max needed no further urging. He shoved her behind the Dumpster, took two running steps and slammed into the door shoulder-first. The lock gave way with a crash that was immediately followed by a flurry of pops and pings, by the scattered sounds of running feet and men's shouts.

"Come on!" Max urged her through the door, pulled a weapon from his coat pocket and fired two shots at their pursuers before following her into the building opposite the hotel.

More relieved than surprised that he was armed, Raine had the quick impression of a neatly ordered storeroom before Max slammed the door, cutting off the outside light. "This way," she said, striking out for the opposite side of the room without waiting for her eyes to adjust. She tripped and stumbled forward, banging her shin into the edge of something solid and metal. She hissed with pain but kept moving, conscious of the men in the alley, of Max's harsh breathing at her side.

What the hell was going on here? People were *shooting* at her. After the bombing, she knew she shouldn't be surprised, but things like this just didn't *happen* to normal people.

She was in way over her head and didn't know how to get back up to the surface.

Footsteps drew closer behind them. The door groaned inward, casting diffuse light into the storeroom. Close. The men were too close!

There! Raine and Max reached for the storeroom door as one, yanking it open and crowding through. They stumbled into a chrome-and-steel space crowded with white-clad bodies and the smells of bread and pastries.

A heavyset man in a bouffant hat yelled, "Hey, where'd you come from? You're not supposed to be here!"

Neither Max nor Raine bothered to answer. They fled, shoving past a line of cooks and barreling through a set of swinging doors into the front area of the bakery. At nearly four-thirty Thursday morning, the area was crowded with people and boxes and fresh baked goods. Max's duffel swung off his shoulder and thumped a startled-looking man, who lost control of his full tray of doughnuts. The doughy disks went flying, adding to the chaos.

Workers scattered with a flurry of screams and shouts. A big man wielding a long bread knife stepped into Raine's path, hands upraised. "Hold it!"

She dodged him as a shot whizzed past her ear and blew out the front window. Max spun and returned fire until his weapon clicked on an empty clip. Bakery employees ran for the exits, clogging the distance that separated the pursued from the pursuers.

Breath sobbing in her lungs, Raine fumbled with the lock and then the door, pushing when she should have pulled. Nearly weeping with exertion, with fear, she got it open and plunged out into the cold night air.

With Max at her heels, she dashed across the sidewalk and darted between two parked cars, but a double-parked vehicle blocked the way.

A big, dark limousine with tinted windows.

"Oh, no!" Raine skidded to a halt and tried to backpedal as a rear door swung open and a man emerged. Raine had a fleeting impression of silver hair, a long, dark coat and polished shoes.

Max slammed into her, then grabbed her when she would have lurched forward. "This way!" he shouted, and pulled her away from the limo and the silver-haired man.

Then they were running, skidding across the icy street in a crazy zigzag pattern. Two shots glanced off a storefront window. A third bullet cracked the safety glass. Max took one look at the window display, where photographs of glittering diamonds flanked empty velvet-covered stands.

Without slackening speed, he ran at the window, slamming his shoulder directly beside the crack.

The safety glass groaned. Sagged. Gave way beneath him.

And all holy hell broke loose. Lights erupted and sirens whooped shrill alien screams.

"Come on!" Max grabbed her hand and

practically dragged her over the waist-high wall and into the jewelry store.

"What are you doing?" She had to yell to be heard over the din.

"Attracting attention. Get down." He pushed her head below window level, waited a moment and then inched up for a look. "Bingo."

He helped Raine up.

The street was empty. The limo had gone.

"We can't trust the cops right now, but we *can* trust that the men who're after you don't want to attract too much attention," Max said with some satisfaction. Then he hefted the duffel that contained his clothing and the sum total of her possessions. "Come on."

This time Raine balked. "Where are we going? And why can't we trust the cops?"

"We're getting the hell out of here so we're not arrested for breaking and entering," he said, boosting her over the wall and following her back onto the street. Then he took her hand and towed her along as he walked briskly down the street.

"As for the rest, I'll tell you once we're in the air."

She nearly had to jog to keep up, but the faint sound of police sirens over the jewelry store alarms had her quickening her steps. "At the risk of repeating myself, where the hell are we going?"

"Philadelphia. We need to talk to Cari Summerton's widower."

Chapter Nine

But once they were in a taxi headed for the airport, Max swore bitterly. "I'm an idiot. We can't fly. They'll be tracking our credit cards and ID." He leaned forward and tapped the driver on the shoulder. When the man had removed his thoroughly illegal headphones, Max said, "Change of plans. Take us to the Amtrak terminal."

Raine wanted to protest, to scream, to demand an explanation. Who were *they?* But the draining adrenaline left her shaky and numb, made her feel as if she were acting rather than reacting. So she let her head drop back on the seat. "We'll need ID to take the train, too."

"That's the plan."

Sure enough, when they got to the train station, which was just opening at 5:00 a.m., he bought two tickets to Boston on his credit card. Then he pocketed the tickets and took her arm. "Come on. There's a car rental place down the street."

There, he rented a high-end sedan using a fake ID and matching credit card, both in the name Mike Walsh. He talked loudly about seeing the Connecticut beaches, asked for directions to the Mystic Seaport, and cuddled close to Raine when the desk clerk was watching.

She remained virtually unresponsive, but inside, the numbness was giving way to a quiet burn of anger.

"Come on, pumpkin. I promised you breakfast by the water, didn't I?" He took her hand and laced his fingers through hers, giving them a squeeze for the benefit of their audience.

She batted her eyelashes and faked a simper, but her voice held an edge when she said, "You certainly did, *honey bear.* Let's hit the road."

The moment they were on I-95 south, headed for Philadelphia, she turned to him.

Before she could speak, he held up a hand. "I owe you some explanations."

"Yes, you do. And we'll get to them in a minute. But before that, I have something to say." Raine took a deep breath, wanting to get this right. "I'm not a victim, Max, and I'm not a damsel in distress. I'm a grown-up and a businesswoman. Maybe when you first got to know me I was someone else, someone I'm not very proud of anymore, but that's not who I really am."

He gave the rearview mirror a long look before he glanced at her. "Let me guess. Ike told you about my Damsel In Distress Syndrome. Did she also tell you about Charlotte?"

"She mentioned the name," Raine said. "But you don't have to talk about her. She doesn't really have anything to do with the two of us."

"Maybe. Maybe not. Hear me out." Max glanced at her, then returned his eyes to the road. "Charlotte reminded me of you in some ways. She was divorced and childless, and had a good job until the company was bought out and they cut her loose with nothing. The job market was tough, so she picked up a few shifts at the hospital gift shop and tried to make it work. That's where I met her." He shrugged. "I noticed the resemblance, but she was completely different from you in other ways. For one, she wanted a husband and kids."

"In other words, she wanted to be a stay-at-home mom." Raine braced herself when he made another high-speed lane change. She wasn't sure whether he was trying to outrun pursuit or something else. "Not that there's anything wrong with that. I respect the choice. It's just not what I'm looking for and we both know it." She let her hand drop to her belly, where Rory's child had once grown. "And it's not that I don't want kids ever. It's just that…" She blew out a breath, frustrated. "How did this get to be about me?"

"It isn't. I was telling you about Charlotte and why I don't do rescues anymore." He paused, then continued, "She moved in with me pretty quickly, maybe too fast, but sometimes these things happen quickly. I helped get her into a nursing program, found her part-time work at the hospital. She was getting on her feet, getting stronger, and…" He shrugged. "It stopped working."

Raine tightened her fingers on the door handle as she remembered what Ike had said. "She didn't need you anymore."

She expected an argument. Instead, he inclined his head. "Maybe. It's taken me a while to admit, but yeah, that's probably part of it. Once her gratitude wore off, we weren't a very good fit. I came home one day and she was gone without a word." He grimaced. "Felt familiar."

"Except that I didn't take off with your furniture. I didn't take anything of yours."

"She took *things*. You took something else."

Unwilling—maybe even unable—to go farther down that path, Raine said, "I didn't mean to. I don't know what I meant to do, but regardless, I didn't handle it well."

"It's over," he said firmly. "And probably for the best. Once your life got itself back on track, you and I would've been a worse fit than Charlotte and I turned out to be. You've already got yourself a family. Rainey Days."

"That's right." But was it, really? Jeff wasn't who she'd thought he was. Tori was a friend, true, but her other employees were acquaintances at best.

Raine was reminded of the melancholy she'd felt while watching the Thriller ad and seeing the love on-screen. Silence stretched thin between them, tense with the things that had been said, with the things that were left yet unsaid. Then Max yanked the wheel, sending the car hurtling out of the high-speed lane without warning.

Raine squeaked and hung on to the door handle as they flew into a rest area going way too fast, bypassed the gas pumps and returned to the highway without stopping.

Max glanced over at her. "Sorry. Just checking for a tail."

"See one?"

"No."

Raine pinched the bridge of her nose

where a tension headache had taken up permanent residence four days earlier. "Then don't you think it's time you told me what the hell happened back at the hotel? Why were those men shooting at us? And who is Charlie?"

He took one hand off the wheel and patted her knee. "Don't worry about it. You're safe with me."

She picked up his hand with her thumb and forefinger, returned it to his side of the car and dropped it in his lap to make the point. "In case you missed the first half of our conversation, we agreed that I'm not a damsel in distress. I'm every bit as much of a functional, capable woman as your Einstein, and I'd appreciate it if you'd treat me as such. You can start by briefing me on my case. Got it?"

That earned her a long, measured look followed by a short nod. "Okay. If you insist." He paused, then said, "Have you ever heard of The Nine?"

"Like from *The Lord of the Rings*?"

"Not quite. Or maybe that's where they got the name, but not the premise. It's a myth." He blew out a breath and contradicted himself. "At least I thought it was a myth. But then my very reliable informant tells me he has evidence that The Nine are behind the Thriller deaths and the attacks on you and me."

A chill skittered through Raine, a sizzle of mingled excitement and dread. Excitement at the thought of identifying a foe. Dread that the case seemed to be growing bigger and more dangerous than either of them had imagined it might. "Tell me more."

He eased up on the gas as they flew past a speed trap, then put the hammer back down when the cop didn't pursue. "Supposedly," he said, "The Nine is a group of very powerful doctors and scientists—exclusively men—who have taken it upon themselves to regulate the progress of the biotech industries. Their resources are rumored to be nearly unlimited."

"That's like something out of a B-rated movie." Raine looked at him, waiting for the punch line. When it didn't come, she said, "It's impossible, right?"

"It should be. But what if it isn't? It never seemed logical that a single enemy could be powerful enough to simultaneously engineer the four Thriller deaths while attempting to frame you, then blowing up the office when it seemed like the frame might not be working."

Raine shivered, though Max had cranked the vehicle's heater up to the highest setting. She was quiet for a moment before she said, "According to Ike, Jeff's sick brother got his transplant last month, paid for by a private benefactor."

Max nodded grimly. "That's consistent with this crazy theory of Charlie's."

"Did he have any proof?" Raine couldn't believe she was even considering this as a valid possibility. That *they* were considering it.

"A data disk. He said I should use it to take down The Nine, that they suppressed a drug that could have saved his wife. I've got Ike looking at it now. She'll call me on the disposable cell when she has something."

"What do you think could be on the disk?"

He shrugged. "Not sure." Then he glanced at her. "But Charlie's day job was acting as an attorney for Pentium Pharmaceuticals."

"Which has a Thriller competitor in the pipeline," Raine said, voice growing grimmer as too many seemingly unrelated pieces of information started to fall into place. Anger surged alongside confusion and she turned to Max. "Why aren't we taking this to Detective Marcus?"

"Because while I think we can trust Marcus, I'm not sure about his superiors, and I have my doubts about Agent Bryce. Besides, all we've got are conjectures based on an urban legend. You think that's going to stand up if someone higher in the system is working to block us? I don't. Worse, the cops still have the data ghosts, which go a long way toward suggesting that you're in on it." He shook his head. "I'm not willing to take the risk."

"In other words, we need to find enough evidence to prove this urban legend regardless of who is applying pressure, then take it to the authorities."

"While also staying ahead of the guys who tried to gun us down earlier," Max added.

Raine thought of the silver-haired guy. "Did you recognize the man who got out of the limo?"

"No, but I'll call Ike with a description. She can do her thing while we're working this end."

"Trying to figure out how and why the dead women were killed." Raine hugged herself. "God, somehow it all seems much more real now that we're talking about the who and why of it." And now that she'd been shot at. The fire and the explosion had been awful, but they had been destructive forces aimed at buildings, not direct attacks.

The early morning chase left no room for debate. Someone wanted her and Max dead.

"Hey," he said, his voice softening a shade. "You're not a victim or a rescue, but I'll protect you anyway. You know that, right?"

A lump pressed unexpectedly in her throat when she nodded. "I know." She would have to make that be enough, for both their sakes. She sniffed back a surge of wistfulness. "And since I'm not a victim or a rescue, I'll expect you to keep me informed and let me be involved in talking to the families."

When he hesitated, she said, "This is my career we're talking about, Max. My life."

Finally, he nodded. "Okay."

She held a hand across the small space. "Partners?"

He snorted. "William wouldn't think much of me replacing him." But he took her hand. Instead of shaking it, he held it for a long moment while his skin warmed hers. Then he squeezed her fingers, sending a fine hint of warmth across her nerve endings, one that intensified when he said, "You got it."

But he didn't say the word, emphasizing what Raine already knew. He would always see her as fragile and in need of protection. Never as his partner.

Never as his equal.

THEY BYPASSED NEW YORK CITY, to avoid both the traffic and the possibility of picking up a tail, on the off chance that the offices of Vasek and Caine were under surveillance. Still, they ran into traffic and it was nearly 10 a.m. before they reached the suburban Philadelphia address Ike had found for James Summerton, the husband of the first reported victim.

When Max had parked in the driveway and shut off the rental car, Raine sat for a moment, gathering her courage.

"You okay?" he asked.

She nodded. "Yes. We need to do this. And it helps knowing that if we find a real explanation for what happened, it might give the victims' families some added peace. Maybe not now, but later."

But still, sick knots coiled in her stomach as they walked past a boxy sedan and followed the neat brick pathway up to a single-level house. The walls were white vinyl, and the shrubs flanking the side door were wrapped in burlap and coated with a layer of ice and snow. The house looked tucked in for the winter, with only the half-mast flag in the front yard and the strip of black bunting across the kitchen window attesting to the recent tragedy.

When Max moved to the door, she waved him back. "I'll do it." She mounted the short flight of stairs and rang the doorbell, hearing it chime inside the house.

There was no response.

She pressed the bell again, then opened the aluminum storm door and knocked on the inner wooden panel. "Mr. Summerton? Anyone home?" Maybe he'd gone to work, she thought, though that seemed odd so soon after his wife's death.

Then she heard a baby's fitful cry. The sound brought back that first phone call and the sound of a man's voice saying, *My wife Cari is dead...she took Thriller...we have a baby.*

God.

Suddenly panicked, Raine turned and stumbled down the steps. Max caught her upper arm in a firm grip. "Running away?"

"No." She stopped as the door opened behind her. "Of course not."

Only she had been about to run, and they both knew it.

"Can I help you?" A man stood on the other side of the door with a cloth slung over his shoulder and a puzzled expression on his face. He was in his late twenties or so, average looking, dark haired and green eyed, wearing decent catalog clothes. He focused on Raine, scanning her from her sensible boots to her jeans and sweater. "Are you from the nanny agency?"

Behind him, the baby's wails escalated rapidly.

Raine stepped forward and raised her voice to be heard over the cries. "Mr. Summerton, I'm Corraine and this is Max." She used her full first name in the hopes that he wouldn't immediately connect her with Rainey Days. "We're with a group that's investigating pharmaceutical-related deaths. I hate to bother you right now, but could we have five minutes of your time?"

While she spoke, his face transformed successively from hopeful to shattered, then wary. "Are you reporters?"

"No," Max said from the bottom step, where he seemed smaller and less imposing than he did on level ground. "We're with Vasek and Caine Investigations." He opened his wallet and pulled out a business card. "Can we come in and ask you a few questions?"

Summerton looked ready to refuse, but just then the baby's cries went silent. He cast a panicked look over his shoulder. "Fine. Shut the door behind you."

Raine entered the house with Max at her heels, and followed James Summerton through the kitchen and into a small sitting room. She got a sense of a tidy, ordered home overlaid with a layer of clutter. Dirty dishes were stacked in the sink and things looked vaguely out of place, as though they'd been put down and forgotten by a man used to his wife picking up after him.

"There she is!" Summerton made a valiant effort to interject joy into his voice, but Raine could see the toll of grief in the slump of his shoulders when he leaned down and plucked a small, pink-clad child from a folding crib. "There's my girl!"

The baby—little more than a year old— looked over his shoulder at the strangers and opened her mouth to howl.

Then she stopped. Smiled. Cooed.

And reached for Raine.

"No, baby. She's here to talk to Daddy." Summerton shifted his grip on the little girl and gestured Raine and Max over to a pretty chintz-covered couch. "Go ahead. Sit." He looked around blankly. "Can I get you anything? I have…" He trailed off. "Hell, I don't know what I have. Cari takes—took care of the entertaining. And the grocery shopping." He looked around again as though expecting her to be there.

"We're fine," Max said quickly. "And we don't want to take up too much of your time. We're just looking to get a sense of your wife's medical history, and maybe some of the events surrounding her passing."

Raine winced at his forthrightness, but it seemed to work on Summerton. He visibly collected himself and shifted his grip on the baby once again as she squirmed, still heading for Raine.

Thwarted, the little girl burst into loud, miserable tears.

"I'm sorry," Summerton said, trying to

shush the baby and looking close to tears himself. "I'm sorry, she misses Cari. Shush, sweetie, it's okay. Daddy's here. I'm sorry."

"Here. Let me." Raine transferred the dribble rag from Summerton's shoulder to her own and plucked the baby from his arms. With motions honed by too many hours of babysitting to count, she perched the child on her shoulder and soothed her with a combination jiggle-bounce and circular back rub.

When the baby quieted, she nodded to a stunned-looking Max. "Go ahead."

He stared at her for a moment longer before he turned to Summerton. "Okay, here goes. What can you tell me about your wife's family medical history? Any heart problems, cancer, high blood pressure, diabetes, that sort of thing?"

Summerton divided his attention between Max and his daughter, who had cuddled right up against Raine's neck. "Cari's mother is staying with me. She'll be back any time now, and could answer that better than I can. But I think she's got an aunt with late-onset Alzheimer's, and her great grandfather died of a heart attack in his forties. Beyond that, nothing that I know of."

"How was Cari's health in general?"

"Good," Summerton said quickly. Then he took a breath. "It was good. She was healthy. A little heavier than she'd been before the baby, but she was working on that. She was a little depressed, I think, because I've been away so much lately and she'd been here alone with the baby...." He shot a look at his daughter, as though fearing she'd overhear and take it the wrong way. "There just hadn't been much time for the two of us, you know?"

Max nodded sympathetically. "Anything problematic about the birth?"

Raine paused in her jiggle-bounce, startled by the question, but he was right. What if all four women had recently given birth? It was definitely something to check out. A risk factor, of sorts.

"Well, she had a C-section. Something about her pelvic conformation wasn't optimal. They said it was the safest way."

When Max nodded encouragingly, Summerton continued, "As long as they had to open her up, Cari got a tummy tuck. She'd been hinting about wanting breast implants recently, but I didn't want her to get them. She's—she *was* perfect already."

His face nearly crumpled, but he pulled it together, and held it together through the remainder of Max's questions. Raine couldn't tell if they were gathering useful information or not, but the baby grew heavy and warm as she dropped off to sleep, in turn relaxing muscles that Raine hadn't even realized were tight.

She leaned her cheek against the pink-clad back and indulged in a moment of baby smell.

Contrary to what Max might think, she didn't have anything against babies. She just didn't think a woman should have one just because she happened to have a uterus. Until she could say without hesitation that she was willing to give up her other goals, or at least put them on hold for twenty years or so, then she didn't feel she was ready for a child of her own.

If she never was, that would be okay, she told herself firmly, ignoring the little ache that fisted beneath her heart when Baby Summerton cooed in her sleep.

"Thanks for your time," Max said. He stood and shook Summerton's hand. "My cell number is on the card, please feel free to call me if you or your mother-in-law think of anything else that might be helpful."

"I will." Summerton looked over to Raine and his eyes softened. "Thank you for taking her. That meant a great deal to both of us."

"Of course." Raine eased the sleeping child off her shoulder and placed her in the crib. She handed Summerton the dribble rag. "She's a beautiful girl."

Still looking down at his sleeping daughter, he nodded. "Yes, she is. I just wish—" He broke off and swallowed hard. "I wish she'd gotten to know her mother."

Eyes filling, Raine mumbled something appropriate, shook Summerton's hand and fled to the rental car. There, she breathed deeply and had herself more or less under control by the time Max joined her.

He started the engine and pulled out of the driveway before he glanced over at her. "That was quite a scene back there."

She wasn't sure if he meant her with the baby, or Summerton talking about his loss, so she went with a noncommittal, "Neither of us expected this to be easy." She took a deep breath. "I'm not sure I expected it to be this hard, though. Even though I know I did everything I could to ensure that Thriller would be safe for its users, I can't help thinking…" She trailed off and stared out the window, throat closing on tired, hopeless tears.

This time, when he took her hand, he simply held it.

Chapter Ten

Though it was only midday, Max could see that Raine was near collapse. He thought about driving through, but he was low on sleep too, so he picked a hotel at random and checked in under a totally bogus name, paying cash from the emergency stash he'd retrieved from the bottom lining of his duffel bag.

With only a few hundred dollars, he thought about saving money by just getting one room. But ever since earlier that day, when he'd opened up to Raine about Charlotte, he'd felt his natural anti-Raine defenses weakening. They'd taken another hard hit when he'd seen her holding Baby

Summerton and something had clicked in his brain, in his gut.

That's what I want, the click had said. *Only that. Only her.*

Too bad he couldn't fully trust the feeling, or the woman. They might make a good couple for a while, but she'd run in the end. That was her pattern, and he didn't see any evidence of it changing.

So he asked for separate rooms without a connecting door. If he was near her, he would only want her. And from the looks he'd intercepted once or twice over the course of the morning, he had a feeling she wanted him right back. But anything they'd have together would be temporary, and he wasn't looking for temporary.

Especially not the kind that took a part of him when it left.

He led the way to the fifth floor and handed her a key card. "I'm right next door. Knock if you need me."

She looked startled for a moment, then her face flooded with a complicated mix of emotions. "Does that mean you trust me not to run?"

"I trust that you're smart enough to know you're safer with me than without me at this point. And I know you're smart enough to figure out you won't get far without using your credit card number, which I can pretty much guarantee has been flagged by both Detective Marcus and The Nine."

He wasn't sure when the existence of the shadow group had gone from impossible to probable in his mind, but too many of the facts fit best when he plugged them into a group rather than a single individual or company.

"Thanks for the vote of confidence, I guess," Raine said, lips twisting in a rueful smile. "I'm going to get some sleep. Want to meet for dinner?"

"I'm going to get room service and keep working." He jammed his key card in the slot with more force than necessary. "I'll call the next-of-kin in Richmond. We'll go there tomorrow morning, then swing back up to the third victim's family in

New York City." Saying it like that brought home a point he'd begun to consider that afternoon.

Apparently Raine caught the connection, too. "Do you think it's significant that three of the four deaths were on the east coast?"

He used his foot to hold open his hotel room door. "I'm not sure, but Ike's checking it out. She's trying to pull the sample batch numbers and see if the deaths were linked that way. Maybe a small portion of the samples were tainted during the original production process."

Raine frowned. "How is she going to figure out…she's hacking into the FDA? That's illegal!"

"So's conspiring to hold useful drugs off the market so your own patented compounds keep making money." Max pushed the door open and stepped through. As an afterthought, he pulled out a twenty from the emergency funds and handed it to Raine. "Get something from room service for yourself." When she shook her head in protest, he insisted, "Trust me, protein and carbs. You may not want to eat, but you'll feel better if you do."

After a pause and a sigh, she took the twenty, lips curving in a soft smile. "You saving me again, Max?"

"Nah. Saving myself from having to carry you around tomorrow after you faint from low blood sugar." That got a small laugh out of her, pleasing Max. Feeling as though they were chitchatting to prolong the end of a date, he said, "Good night. Sleep well."

And before he'd fully processed the impulse, he leaned down and kissed her softly on the lips.

It was a chaste kiss, little more than he might give a first date he hadn't really connected with. But its effect on Max was anything but chaste.

His blood leaped in his veins, revving from idle to racing speed between one heartbeat and the next. Her lips yielded beneath his, warm and inviting, and he was poised to accept that invitation—

When she pulled away.

She blinked up at him, then exhaled a

long breath. "Sorry, Max. I'm not looking to be rescued anymore, and I don't want a man who has to be needed that way. I'm looking for someone who'll see me as an equal, someone who'll need me as much as I need him."

I see you as an equal, he started to say, but stopped when he realized that wasn't so. He saw her as a beautiful, desirable woman. As the surprisingly savvy boss of a company that had proved itself successful up until its current troubles. As a different person than the vulnerable, fragile woman he'd known back in Boston.

But not as his equal. Not as someone he could turn to when things got tough.

She nodded. "Thought so." She pressed her lips together as though remembering his kiss. "Too bad, Max. It might've been fun for a while."

She disappeared into her room next door, leaving him alone with the taste of her on his lips.

"WHEW. NARROW ESCAPE," Raine said into the generic hotel room, the likes of which were becoming depressingly familiar. She glanced around, saw nothing out of the ordinary and shrugged. "Guess it's a shower first."

Then she stopped, having realized that she was talking to herself, trying to fill the quiet. She'd been in constant company for nearly the past four days.

Being alone felt strange. A little eerie.

"Max is right next door. There's even a connector." She crossed the room and unlatched her side, so he could come through if she called for him. Not that she would, of course, but in the case of an emergency...

"Get a grip," she told herself. "They don't know where we are. You're safe here."

Still, the creepy feeling persisted as she checked and double checked the locks, then stripped down for her shower.

She was tempted to luxuriate beneath the spray, but that felt somehow wrong after what she'd been through that day. Cari Summerton would never again take a good shower, would she? That sweet little girl would never get to swim with her mother, never get to talk to her, laugh with her, yell at her, all those things girls did when they grew up with a mother of their own.

Many of the things Raine had missed out on.

"This isn't about you," Raine said sternly as she shut off the water and stepped out onto the bathmat. "None of it is about you. At least not directly."

It was about Thriller. About a group of men who, for reasons unknown, had decided to discredit the drug and destroy her in the process.

Collateral damage, Ike had called it.

When self-pity threatened, Raine scrubbed harder at her hair, wringing it dry until the tears came from the pull at her scalp rather than worthless sniveling. She wrapped a dry towel around her torso and stepped out into the hotel room.

And stopped. "Oh, hell." Her relatively clean clothes—the business outfit she'd washed in the sink last night and hung to dry—were in Max's duffel. She looked down at herself. "Oh, hell no. That's so not happening."

Refusing to be so stupid—or obvious—as to visit Max in a hotel-size towel, she grimaced and pulled the jeans and sweater back on. She padded to the connecting door barefoot and knocked.

She heard the sound of a lock being thrown, and the door swung open to reveal a scowling Max. "There wasn't supposed to be a connecting door."

Though she felt a frisson of disappointment at how thoroughly he wanted to avoid her, Raine shrugged. "Sorry. I promise not to bother you again. I need my clothes."

His face went blank. Then comprehension washed over his expression. "Right. Wait here." He turned away, cursed and turned back. "Ignore me, I'm being an ass. Come in." He gestured to a table beneath the single window, where a room service tray rested. "Eat. I got enough for two, because I figured you wouldn't follow orders."

"I just got out of the shower!" But even given the circumstances, Raine found a faint smile. "It's one of the basic differences between men and women. The woman showers first. The man orders food."

Still standing, they shared a tentative smile.

At Max's prompting, she sat. Their knees bumped beneath the hotel-issue table, but neither of them mentioned the contact.

Many things went unspoken as the meal progressed.

By silent accord, they kept the conversation light. They didn't speculate on the case. They didn't talk about their past association or the way it had ended. They didn't talk about Charlotte or Max's empty apartment. Raine didn't ask whether he'd ever gone to New Bridge, looking for her once she'd run.

Instead, they stuck to safe stuff like movies—which they mostly agreed on—books—ditto—and the occasional foray into current affairs and politics, where they were forced to agree to disagree.

The good news was that it made for a pleasant meal. The bad news was that it recalled entirely too many of the hours they'd shared during her stay at Boston General.

Worse, it reminded her that Max wasn't

just a handsome face stuck on a hell of a body. He wasn't just an overprotective macho man in search of a little woman to take care of.

He was both of those things, true.

But he was also really good company, damn it.

When the meal was over, their conversation faltered. She fell silent, and after a moment, he did, too. They stared at each other over the remains of their food. The scene was lit by daylight filtering through cheap hotel curtains. It wasn't romantic, wasn't ambience, but Raine's heart tilted nonetheless.

"Aw, hell." Max leaned forward and Raine met him halfway. Their kiss tasted of red wine and companionship, and the heat built gently. Surely. As though this time it was right.

Only it wasn't. He'd already admitted he didn't see her as an equal.

He was still looking to save her.

Raine pulled away, blood humming, and saw the knowledge already written in his eyes.

"Not yet," he said as though they'd already discussed it. "Not tonight."

Maybe not ever. Probably not ever.

"Thanks for the meal." Raine stood and gathered her change of clothes. "See you tomorrow."

She surprised herself by sleeping through the afternoon and night, and she woke with the taste of him on her lips.

THE ADDRESS IKE HAD GIVEN THEM in Richmond, Virginia, belonged not to a family member of the second victim, Minifred Tyrrel, but to her former roommate, Jenni, a late twentysomething who died her hair platinum blond and wore her pants two sizes too small.

She had agreed to meet with them at noon. When she opened the door, she took one look at Max and couldn't have been more helpful.

"Minni was on the pill," she said, inching a little closer to Max on the love seat she'd insisted they both use, leaving Raine on the big couch by herself.

Max forced himself to hold his ground

and continue with the questions as though her stocking-clad foot wasn't taking a leisurely tour of his inseam. "Any other meds? What about recreational drugs?"

"A little X. Maybe some pot now and then. Nothing hard-core." She glanced at the kitchen, overtly ignoring Raine. "Can I get you anything?"

"No, I'm fine," Max answered, leery of what she might offer. "Did Minni smoke or drink?"

"She drank some. Nothing heavy-duty. And she used to smoke, but she quit right before she got her nose done. The doctors said it would screw up the healing."

"True enough." As he kept going with the questions—mostly gleaned from basic medical history reports, with a few oddball-risk factors Ike and Raine had come up with—Max took a look around the third-floor apartment. It was cramped and vaguely seedy, though one of the girls had made an effort to pretty the place up by draping brightly colored scarves over the lamps and tacking travel posters across the more obvious cracks in the drywall.

By the time they'd gotten to Minni's eating habits—and Jenni's foot had cruised past Max's knee—Raine interrupted, "No offense, Jenni, but you don't seem too broken up by your roommate's death."

"We weren't tight." As though realizing that sounded bitchy, she quickly said, "And I'm on antidepressants."

Which made it all better, apparently.

Max ran her through the rest of the questions at lightning speed, and he and Raine escaped into the early afternoon air of Virginia.

They made it to the car before they looked at each other and burst out laughing.

"Her foot was...it was..." Raine pointed and dissolved into giggles.

"I know exactly where it was, thank you," Max said, still chuckling. "And where it was going."

Their laughter drained quickly, but it had boiled off some of the tension between them as they pulled back onto the road, headed for New York City and the parents of the third victim, Denise Allen.

The disposable cell phone rang just before they reached the Virginia border. He answered. "What have you got for me?"

"I think I've got a few things you'll be interested in hearing," Ike's voice said, sounding far away.

"Tell me." The cheap plastic creaked when his fingers tightened on the casing, but the disposable phones were the only safe method of communication. There was too good a chance that their regular numbers were being monitored.

Raine mouthed, *Is that Ike?* When Max nodded, she gestured for him to hold the phone away from his ear and leaned close so she could listen in.

Ike said, "First off, I've tracked down the sample batch information for the four dead women, to see when the pills that—allegedly—killed them were manufactured. Two came from the same batch, but the other two don't come close to matching, which seems to rule out the possibility that one or two batches were somehow contaminated during the production process."

"That's good news for Rainey Days, but

doesn't help the investigation a whole lot," Max said.

"There's more. Agent Bryce actually made pretty good progress before the explosion. Although the dead women don't appear to overlap in terms of their doctors, hospitals or medical conditions, the FDA records show that all four sample batches were distributed at a trade show attached to a big medical conference last month."

"We had reps there," Raine confirmed. "It was one of our promotional pushes."

There was a pause, and Max expected Ike to say something about Raine being on the line. Instead, she continued with her report, voice more subdued than it had been. "Granted, Rainey Days' records show that the samples were only distributed in a limited number of venues, but it does seem suspicious. It's possible some of the samples were subjected to adverse conditions during the trade show—heat or contact with another chemical or something."

"Or maybe that was where The Nine met to engineer their plan," Max said grimly.

"Make a theory to fit the evidence, Vasek," Ike cautioned. "Don't twist the evidence to fit your theory. But yeah, it plays both ways."

Raine spoke up. "Was there anything else in the FDA files? Anything on the data ghosts?"

"Nothing," Ike said flatly. "It looks like the investigation had been more or less shut down, though they're waiting on the DNA information of the bombing victim. They have their suspect, and Detective Marcus had a judge issue a warrant for your arrest."

Raine recoiled from the phone, face going sickly pale.

Max reached over and squeezed her knee. "That doesn't change anything important." Except that now they were trying to avoid both the cops and The Nine. He returned his attention to the phone. "What else do you have for us? Anything on that disk Charlie gave me?"

Max felt a dig of remorse that he'd fled the murder scene, but reminded himself that they'd go to the authorities as soon as they had the evidence to back up their admittedly wild theory.

Nobody would buy into it otherwise.

"I was able to confirm that he lost his wife to cancer last year. I couldn't find the wonder drug that was supposedly suppressed, but get this—the disk he gave you was a conference room surveillance video from his own law firm. Seems like they tape their meetings—wonder if the clients know? Anyway, there are two men on the clip—one is the managing partner, Niles Brant. The other fits the description you gave me last night of the man you saw get out of the limo the other night. The audio's corrupted, so I don't have anything of the conversation yet. I know a guy who knows a guy who might be able to help us, though."

Max cursed the delay. "Any idea who the second man is?"

"Working on it. He doesn't seem to belong to any of the big drug companies. I'm thinking I'll show the picture around Boston General today. If he's a local and he's in the medical or biotech fields, someone should know him."

"Be careful," Max warned.

"Yes, Dad." But Ike's tone was serious when she said, "I'm headed to the Cape for the weekend with a friend, but I'll bring the laptop and keep this phone. Call if you really need me."

"Hot date?"

"Hot enough," she answered with a thread of amusement in her voice. "But I'm here if you need me."

"Thanks Ike, I owe you one."

"Just take care of yourself and we'll call it even," she said, and he knew she wasn't just talking about the possibility of an attack.

She hung up before he could respond.

Max folded the phone shut and tucked it into his pocket before glancing at Raine. She was too pale, too quiet.

"Hey," he said softly. "I mean it. The warrant doesn't change anything substantial. We're working the case. We'll figure it out and pull together enough evidence that they can't possibly charge you." He wanted to touch her again, but kept both hands on the steering wheel. "I won't let them put you in jail. If they do, I'll bust you out, okay?"

She stirred, forcing a weak smile at the joke. "That's one rescue I'll hold you to, Vasek." She looked down at her hands. "It's not the warrant. Or not just the warrant. It's everything." Her gesture encompassed the vehicle, the passing scenery and the two of them. "On Monday I was sitting in my office with two of my most trusted employees watching the first of the Thriller ads debut on national TV. Now it's Friday and I'm a fugitive, thanks to one of those trusted employees. I've got no home, no office, and quite possibly no way to fix either of those things." She shrugged. "I've got nothing."

"You've got me," he said without thinking.

The words hung motionless for a few heartbeats, then sank with a sigh.

Chapter Eleven

Raine was exhausted by the time they pulled off at a hotel outside New York City rather than fight the weekend traffic. She'd done little more than sit in rental cars— they'd switched from the sedan to a pickup truck near D.C.—for the past few days, but her bones ached and her joints pinged a protest when she dropped down from the vehicle.

She must have groaned, because Max chuckled softly. "Come on. You hit the shower and I'll order food."

Max rented two rooms and they met in his for dinner without even discussing it. Still bone-tired, though less achy after her shower, Raine headed back to her room after nearly falling asleep in her rubbery room service pasta.

This time, though, there was no goodnight kiss.

As Raine lay in bed, rapidly fading toward sleep, she realized it was because they had reached a plateau of sorts, or maybe a pinnacle. One more kiss, one more touch might unbalance their equilibrium and send them hurtling down one side of the mountain or the other.

She snorted into the darkness, which smelled of cheap hotel. "And the award for the worst metaphor of the night goes to… Raine Montgomery!"

But thinking of her and Max was better than thinking of a warrant with her name on it. Easier than thinking of Baby Summerton, or a girl named Minni whose "kin" hadn't mourned her death.

Simpler than thinking about what came next.

THE FOLLOWING MORNING, they set off just after eight. Max had pushed the schedule back because he was familiar with the city, and figured traffic shouldn't be too awful on a Saturday morning.

A rolled cement truck on the bridge meant they didn't get to the stately old brick home until near 10:00 a.m. There, they found a computer-generated flier pinned to the door.

"Memorial services start at ten," Raine read, then frowned. "The examiners released Denise Allen's body awfully quick, didn't they?" Then she winced. "I'm sorry. That came out harsher than I meant it to."

"Valid point, though." Max frowned at the flier, which offered directions to a nearby church. "Either they're holding a memorial now and planning the burial for later, or someone leaned on the morgue to expedite processing." He glanced over at her. "I'm betting on the latter."

Her eyes had gone hollow in her face. "We should go to the service."

Though he'd been thinking the same thing, Max wished there were another way. Raine was doing her best, but the interviews were taking a toll. She'd become more and more withdrawn as the days had passed.

Regardless of whether it was toxicity or murder, four innocent women had died because of her drug.

Before he could say anything, she shot him a look. "Don't coddle me, Vasek. I'm fine."

He nodded shortly. "Let's head over to the memorial, then."

Despite what most television cop dramas suggested, Max had no hope that the killer would be sitting in a back pew. But the gathering might give them access to friends and family members who might have additional information on Denise's lifestyle.

There had to be a pattern somewhere. A risk factor. A reason the women had died.

Or been killed.

The church was a few blocks from the Allens' stately home. It, too, spoke with the quiet undertones of old money, which was evident in the profusions of fresh off-season flowers and the plush cloth of the bolsters and curtains. Vivid stained glass windows showed scenes of sin and redemption and God's forgiveness, and the air carried the scents of incense and lilies.

Max drew a deep breath and felt something loosen in his chest. Though he had attended church less and less frequently over the past few years, the sounds and sights and smells reminded him of childhood services. Most of the neighborhood congregation had been related to him in one way or another, and the services had been simple and easy for his younger self to understand.

Honor thy family and neighbors. Protect those weaker than yourself. Do no harm.

It was the last two he kept getting stuck on when it came to Raine, he thought as they took a pew six rows from the back so as not to disturb the seated mourners or the memorial, which was already in progress.

A closed casket of polished wood sat at the front of the room, draped with flowers. An enlarged photograph of a woman in her mid-thirties sat atop the flowers, propped up so the mourners could see Denise Allen as she'd been in life.

A podium stood to the left of the casket; a man in cleric's robes stepped away from the microphone and gestured a tall, gray-suited man forward.

Gray Suit leaned too close to the microphone, eliciting a hum of feedback when he started to speak. He eased away and tried again. "I know it might seem strange for me to eulogize my ex-wife, but just because we were divorced doesn't mean we didn't love each other anymore. Let me give you an example." He launched into a rambling story about the gym workouts he and Denise had apparently shared until her death. The longer he spoke, the more he used the word *I* and the less he actually said about his ex-wife.

"Nice guy," Max muttered. He glanced over at Raine, saw her fidget uncomfortably in her seat. Leaning close, he asked, "Are you okay?"

"Sorry. Churches give me the creeps."

Before Max could ask why, a tall, willowy woman with ash-blond hair and a feminine black suit leaned into their pew. "Is there room for one more?"

"Yes. Please join us." Raine scooted over until the edge of her tailored business pants brushed up against Max's jeans.

The woman glanced at their casual clothing, but didn't comment. She faced forward for a minute before she grimaced and whispered, "He's so full of it." She turned to Raine and mouthed, "Don't you think so?"

Raine made a noncommittal noise. "I don't know him well."

"You must know Denise from the shelter, then?"

"Something like that."

Max gave Raine points for playing it off so casually, though he did get a kink of amusement that the woman had apparently placed them in the soup kitchen Ike had noted as one of Denise Allen's regular haunts. Then again, he supposed three days of doing laundry in hotel sinks hadn't done his and Raine's wardrobes any favors.

The blonde leaned closer and confided, "Doug is a real piece of work. As you can see, he likes to be the center of attention." She gestured to the front of the room, where the speaker appeared to be suppressing tears as he talked about how much the divorce had affected him. "I'm surprised he's up there, though. I would've thought he'd be hiding out."

That got Max's attention. "Why is that?"

The blonde's eyes flicked to him. "Because Denise wasn't using the jazz juice with him, that's why. She was at a party with me."

"Jazz juice?" Max prompted, aware that Raine had gone still.

The woman's lips curved. "That's what we call it, anyway. It was Denise's idea—Thriller dissolved in champagne. Double the bubbles."

Oh, hell, Max thought. What if the other dead women had mixed the drug with alcohol and there had been an adverse interaction of the molecule?

Could it be that simple?

Beside him, Raine relaxed and shook her head almost imperceptibly. He took that to mean her people had already tested the Thriller-alcohol interaction for toxicity and found nothing.

"You were both drinking jazz juice that night? Did you get the samples from the same place?" Max kept his voice low, but he was aware that their conversation was starting to attract annoyed looks from the other mourners scattered in the back of the church.

"Sure. Our plastic surgeon, Dr. Moyer." She paused and confided, "Well, he was my plastic surgeon, though I'm not telling what he did. Denise was scheduled for breast implants in the spring. I think she canceled a couple of weeks ago, though, thanks to the jazz juice."

Max stiffened as the connection hit him. He and Raine traded a look. *Plastic surgery.*

Was it a coincidence?

Or was it a risk factor?

"Why did she cancel the appointment?" Raine asked, voice casual, fingers knotted together in her lap.

The blonde shrugged and whispered, "She was kind of insecure about her body, you know? Especially after the way *that one*—" she indicated Doug-the-ex with a jerk of her thumb "—treated her. She thought bigger breasts would make her feel sexier. Then we got those Thriller samples and she decided she didn't need the boobs anymore." The blonde's eyes darkened. "We never thought it'd kill her. There weren't any warnings or anything. If we'd known…"

She trailed off as a sober-faced man in white robes leaned into their pew. "I'm sorry, but I'm going to have to ask you to either be quiet or take this conversation outside. This is a memorial service."

"Of course. Our apologies." Max rose and gestured for Raine to precede him. He nodded at the few people who turned and glared, and felt a beat of remorse for having brought the investigation into the church.

But he couldn't regret the decision. They had their break.

Once they were outside, Raine grabbed his sleeve. "Cari had a tummy tuck after her C-section and wanted breast implants. Jenni had a nose job. Denise also wanted breast implants." Then she frowned. "But unless they were all on some sort of pre- or post-op drug regimen, I can't see how being scheduled for plastic surgery could explain why they died from taking Thriller."

He led the way back to their rented truck, brain humming. "There's one way to test our theory." He reached into his pocket, pulled out the disposable phone and Ike's computer printout, and dialed a number off the paper. He paused on the sidewalk when the connection went through. "Hello? Mrs. Pawcheck? My name is Maximilian Vasek, and I'm with a pharmaceutical investigation firm on the east coast. If you'll allow me, I'd like to ask you a quick question about your daughter, Melissa."

There was a moment of silence before the response came. "Melissa is dead." The woman's voice broke on the words.

"I know and I'm very sorry, Mrs. Pawcheck. I'm one of the people involved in figuring out what happened and making sure the guilty parties are punished."

He heard a sniffle and a gulp, then, "Ask your question."

"Did Melissa ever have cosmetic surgery, or was she planning on having cosmetic surgery in the near future?" Max nearly crossed his fingers, waiting for the answer.

"Yes." The woman's voice was puzzled. "She had an endoscopic brow lift and liposuction last year. Why? Did that have something to do with her death?"

"That's what I'm trying to figure out," Max said, sending Raine a nod. When Mrs. Pawcheck pressed for an elaboration, he ended the call, saying, "We'll let you know as soon as we do, ma'am. Thank you so much for your help."

He snapped the phone shut and gestured for Raine to keep walking. "Brow lift and liposuction last year."

She pressed her lips together. "I guess that means we're onto something."

They just didn't know what yet.

RAINE DROVE THE LAST LEG of their journey so Max could use his phone to touch base with Ike. The unspoken hope was that she'd already found the missing link between plastic surgery and the Thriller deaths.

As she sent the truck along I-95 into Connecticut, Raine thought how strange it felt to be in her home state again. Had it really only been two days since they'd driven to Philadelphia and seen James Summerton? It felt like so much longer.

Max cursed as he dialed Ike's number on the disposable phone for the third time.

"Still nothing?" Raine guessed.

He shook his head. "Maybe her phone crapped out. They're not the sturdiest things on the planet."

But he drummed his fingers on the armrest for a moment, then dialed another number. After punching in a code, he sat back and made a satisfied noise. "She left a message on my home machine."

He cranked the volume on the cell phone and held the unit out so they could both hear Ike's voice say, "I couldn't get through on the disposable and I'm headed off to the Cape, so here goes. The second man in the video is Dr. Frederic Forsythe, a very high-end cosmetic surgeon from—get this—Beverly Hills." Max and Raine shared a look as the message continued. "Forsythe has a place north of Boston where he keeps a string of polo ponies and does the foxhunting thing. That might explain what he's doing in a Boston law firm. We'll see. My buddy's buddy managed to unscramble some of the audio— he's couriering it to our usual spot. I'm sending a care package as well, though there's nothing in it that you don't already know. I'm off for the weekend, but I'll be on the cell if you need me. Ciao."

The message ended with a click, leaving Max frowning through the windshield. Ahead of them, the sky was an ugly purple-gray, signaling that they were driving into the snow squalls promised by the radio news.

"A Beverly Hills plastic surgeon might fit with our hypothesis," Raine said. "Rich. Powerful. Do you think he could be one of The Nine?"

"Maybe." Max nodded. "Possibly." Then he cursed. "But it's still not enough. We need solid evidence, damn it. Without something tangible, we can't go to the authorities."

"There's still the tape from the law office. Maybe the audio will give us something to go on. What did Ike mean by your 'usual place'?"

He shot her an unreadable look. For a moment, she thought he wasn't going to tell her. Then he shrugged. "Logan Airport. The bartenders at Thursday's Restaurant know Ike, and they don't mind stashing stuff for her to pass off to clients now and then. You sit down, order a gin and tonic with an olive, then complain when it doesn't come with an umbrella." He muttered under his breath, "Makes me think Ike and Charlie went to the same spy school."

"What?"

"Nothing."

They drove in silence a while longer, the miles unrolling beneath the wheels of the rented truck. When a green-and-white sign warned that the exit for New Bridge was a few miles up the road, Raine said, "Are we stopping here or heading to Boston?"

If anyone had told her a week earlier that she'd be spending Saturday night in Boston with Max Vasek, she would've thought they were crazy.

He glanced at her, and one corner of his mouth lifted in a rueful half smile. "Ironic how things have come almost full circle, huh?"

"Boston it is, then." She didn't stop to analyze the emotions that crowded her head and her heart. She just cut the wheel, hit the gas and shot out into the passing lane.

A silver sedan did the same three cars back.

Come to think of it, she could swear she'd seen the same car in her rearview mirror several times since they'd passed the Connecticut border.

Raine's gut clenched. "Max. Check out the light gray car behind us."

He twisted around in his seat, reaching for his parka and the weapon he'd reloaded with his last clip of ammo. "We got ourselves a tail?"

"I'm not sure. Maybe." Going on instinct, she cut across two lanes of traffic, aiming for the nearest off-ramp, but not taking it. The low-slung silver car copied the maneuver.

They were being followed.

She gripped the steering wheel with suddenly clammy palms. "How did they find us? We're not even driving the same car we were when we left!" Her voice edged upward in growing panic. "And damn it, I'm driving!"

"Okay, here's what we're going to do." Max's tone was even. Soothing. "You stand up in your seat, but keep your foot on the gas and your hands on the wheel. I'm going to slide underneath you so we can switch without stopping."

"That only works on TV!"

"Well, it'll work for us, too."

Raine bit her lip and stood up until the top of her head neared the roof of the truck. The speedometer edged toward eighty as they flew toward where the road disappeared beneath the ominous line of storm clouds.

The silver car loomed larger in the side mirror. "They're getting closer! And it looks like it's snowing up ahead. That could be a problem."

"There's enough traffic around, we should be safe for right now. They proved earlier that they still want to keep this fairly low profile." He unbuckled his belt and slid across the bench seat, easing an arm beneath and around her. "As for the snow, look at it this way. We've got four-wheel drive. They don't."

"Then—"

A shot exploded through the plastic slider at the rear of the truck cab.

Raine screamed, but kept her foot on the gas. Max ducked, slid back to the passenger side and drew his weapon. "Guess you're driving," he shouted over the sudden rush of wind through the broken slider. "Get us into that storm!"

"I thought you said they wouldn't make a scene in public!"

"I was wrong." His face could have been carved from granite as he steadied the muzzle of his handgun, aiming through the broken window. "They're getting desperate."

"Maybe they found out that we know about Forsythe and the plastic surgery connection." Raine swerved around a slow-moving station wagon. "But how?"

The sedan drew closer. A bullet pinged off the roof of the truck, its momentum spent.

The highway took a long, slow curve that nearly sent them in the opposite direction, then made a sharper bend back toward the storm. Raine gunned the truck through that second turn, took one look at the mess in front of her and stifled a scream.

Ahead of them by no more than a half mile, the sky was an ugly dark gray and the pavement went from tar to slush. Brake lights flared where traffic was stalled by a spin out two-car accident.

"There's no way through!" she said, easing up on the gas pedal.

Max snapped off a shot that had the silver car dropping back a few lengths. "You'll have to find a way. We're low on options."

Her heart jammed into her throat. "I can't."

He leaned back against the dashboard so she could see his face, so she could see he was serious when he said, "You can do it, Raine. I know you can. You're tough and resourceful, and I'm proud to call you my partner."

The words took a moment to penetrate, a moment to warm her from head to toe. Time seemed to slow as ice pellets peppered the windshield like blowing sand.

Seconds turned to minutes as her heart expanded with the knowledge that she wasn't the passive doormat who'd married Rory or clung to Max in the hospital. She *was* tough and resourceful.

And Max saw her as his equal.

Then a bullet whistled through the broken window and plowed into the dashboard. Shards of hard plastic burst outward. One scored Raine's knuckles, and the pain and the sight of blood sped everything up until the world was moving at normal speed again.

Then faster than normal.

A few hundred feet ahead, cars were

stopped all across four travel lanes. The accident took up part of the slow lane and part of the breakdown lane, leaving a narrow gap between a dented Ford and the guardrail. The occupants of the two cars had moved things to the far side of the guardrail, where a small knot of people had clustered and appeared to be arguing over paperwork.

"Hang on!" Making a snap decision, the only one she *could* make, Raine stood on the brakes, slowed the truck to a crawl and dropped it into four-wheel drive while the sedan's driver closed the gap with merciless speed. Then she hit the gas, slalomed between two slowing buses and changed lanes with mere feet to spare.

She aimed for the gap between the accident and the guardrail, leaned on the horn and prayed.

Other horns blared. Tires squealed, then stopped squealing as the moving traffic passed into the snow squall and the surface beneath the tires went from black to white. From traction to none.

Raine felt the truck skid and steered into

the motion, hoping it would be enough. She heard Max fire three times in rapid succession. They were going nearly forty when she threaded the gap between the disabled car and the guardrail, fifty by the time she'd steered back into the travel lanes, where the other cars were creepy-crawling in the snow.

"Hang on, baby, hang on!" she chanted to the truck, feeling the wheels spin and bite.

Max aimed. Fired. And made a low sound of satisfaction. "Gotcha."

Raine glanced in the rearview mirror just in time to see the silver car swerve across the two higher speed lanes, listing on a flat tire. It bounced off the Jersey barriers that separated the south and north-bound lanes of I-95, and ricocheted back into the middle lane, directly into the path of a lumbering casino bus.

The bus clipped the sedan's rear corner, sending it caroming back across the slower lanes. The car skidded sideways and fetched up against the guardrail, then was lost to sight as the highway curved and Raine and Max fled down the nearly empty road.

A few miles later, he pulled out the disposable phone. "Here goes nothing." He punched in a number and waited, tension vibrating through his frame. After a moment, his breath whooshed out. "Ike. Thank God. Listen good and listen fast. I think they're tracking the phones—I don't know how, but the signal is compromised. Dump yours and run. Take the weekend away like you planned, but do it somewhere else. No reservations, no trail. Use cash. Leave me a hint at the usual place. And be careful."

He ended the call, rolled down the window and tossed the phone.

"Ike can look out for herself," Raine said, wanting to ease the grim expression on his face.

Without looking at her, he reached across the bench seat, took her hand and squeezed. "That's right. And we'll look out for each other. The Nine aren't going to know what hit them."

THEY DROVE ANOTHER HOUR in silence before Raine pulled the truck off the highway and into a crowded motel parking lot. "Are we ditching the truck or keeping it?"

"We'll have to keep it," Max answered. "I'm getting low on cash, and I don't think we want to add grand theft auto to our laundry list. At least not until we're sure what we're dealing with."

"Sounds like a plan." Raine parked in a far corner, away from the lights, backing into the spot so the shattered rear slider wasn't so obvious. "We should plan to be up and out before dawn tomorrow." She grabbed the duffel bag out of the truck, tossed Max his jacket, pocketed the keys and slammed the driver's door. "Let's go check in."

When he didn't follow, she stopped and turned back. "Did I forget something?"

Snow feathered down between them, glowing orange in the sodium lights of the parking lot. The contrast made Max seem even larger and darker than he was, but rather than fear, the sight sent a bolt of warmth through Raine's midsection, where it buzzed alongside chase-pumped adrenaline.

A slight smile touched his lips. "You trying to rescue me, partner?"

Something clicked in her chest, right beneath her heart, and suddenly it was so simple to cross to him, stand on her tiptoes and kiss him.

There was no withdrawal this time, only joy, and a feeling that now, finally, he needed something from her. Reassurance. Comfort.

Love.

They kissed as the snow coated the world around them and their bodies went from cold to warm.

That first moment of contact, of acceptance spun into endless minutes as he spanned her waist and slid his hands to the small of her back, then upward, trailing his fingertips over her ribs beneath the ratty brown jacket liner she still wore. She kissed him deeper, stroking her tongue across his, then mimicking the rhythm in the caress of her fingers on the hard planes of his chest.

She murmured his name. "Max."

When they drew apart, they both knew

it was only a temporary thing. And when they stopped at the desk, it was to rent a room with nearly the last of their cash.

One room. No discussion.

Bet Me

When Max, a man who hated hotels, offered to spend an entire weekend in the hotel of Raine's choosing, she knew something big was about to happen.

Chapter Twelve

When the hotel room door closed behind them, Max dropped the bag of sodas and snacks they'd bought at the gift shop in the absence of room service. He held out a hand to Raine.

Heat suffused her body and she crossed to him, knowing it was time. Their time.

They kissed, meeting as equals. Needing each other equally.

He drew away to look down at her with eyes that were dark, and full of fire and promises. Then he released her and stepped away, keeping only her hand, which he raised to his lips. He pressed a kiss to her knuckles. "The first moment I saw you, I thought you were the most beautiful woman I'd ever seen."

The words carried an unexpected punch that caught her beneath the heart and wouldn't let go.

She'd been complimented before. She'd been romanced. But she'd never been thoroughly undone by either.

Not until now.

Until Max.

On another night, with another man, she might have returned the compliment, or slid into the slow tug of desire when he touched his lips to her knuckles a second time. But it was this night with this man.

The man she loved.

The realization was painless, comfortable, as though it had been at the edges of her brain for longer than just this week, waiting for her to figure it out, for them to figure it out and find a way to meet, not as rescued and rescuer, but as partners.

I love you, she thought. She didn't say it aloud, not yet. But she stepped into him, basking in his warmth, in the warmth they created together as she lifted her hands to the buttons of his flannel shirt, which was worn and torn from the trials of the past few days, but still soft against her skin.

He froze, barely breathing as she eased the buttons free, until the shirt hung open, baring a narrow strip of taut male skin, lightly dusted with wiry hair.

Then she looked up at him. "When I knocked at your apartment Tuesday evening, I was thinking about Thriller, and about how I was going to convince you to help me. Then you opened the door, looking just like you do now, and I thought…" She trailed off, throat tightening with the huge emotion of it, clogging to the point that she almost couldn't breathe.

She halfway expected him to go with a quip, with the easy, shared laughter that would defuse a situation that had suddenly grown far heavier than she'd expected, far more serious than she was prepared for. Instead, he took her hands and twined their fingers together. "What did you think?"

"That I'd been stupid."

"To leave Boston?"

She shook her head. "No, to think that I'd forgotten you once I did."

He looked at her for a long moment, perhaps wondering if that was enough when it felt like too much. Then, as though he'd seen an answer she hadn't meant to give, he nodded once, released her hands and shrugged out of his shirt.

A small sound escaped from between Raine's lips at the sight of his bare chest, at the feel of his naked skin beneath her palms.

He kissed her, holding nothing back. She could feel it in the possessive stroke of his hands, in the hard press of his body against hers, centered desire to desire. She could taste his growing impatience, feel the rising heat that met and mated with the rhythmic pound of her blood, the deep-seated pulse in her core.

She was wet for him, weeping for him, aching in places that were familiar yet not, as though her sensuality had awoken from a long, torpid hibernation and was hungry and ready to feed on sex, on Max.

Only Max.

She traced the hard planes of his chest with fingers that trembled with urgency, and maybe a touch of fear. The burgeoning emotions were bigger than she'd expected, huger than she was prepared to face, but there was no turning back now.

Max's skin was a warm slick over hard muscles that coiled and relaxed beneath her touch as he drew her closer, or maybe that was her moving, she wasn't sure. All she knew was that they were wrapped together, twined together until it was difficult to tell where he left off and she began.

She broke the kiss to lay claim to the skin at his throat, which was faintly abrasive with his growing beard, faintly salty with the events of the day. He hummed his approval and dropped his hands to the hem of her shirt, easing it up and over her head so smoothly she barely lost contact with him.

Then it was all contact. Skin to skin. Heartbeat to heartbeat.

He unsnapped her bra and cast it aside, then stepped back until they were facing each other across the hotel room. He looked like a god, clothed in jeans below and nothing above. The dull light of a single lamp softened the planes of his face, making him look less fierce. More approachable.

All but his eyes, which were fixed on her with an almost frightening intensity.

Raine looked down at herself, at her breasts and the smooth skin of her belly. On any other day she might have flushed and tried to cover herself. But now, with this man, she stood fast and grew warm under his inspection. Then, inwardly amazed at her own boldness, she touched the button at the waistband of her tailored slacks. "I've thought of us doing this, too many times to count."

At the flare of heat in his eyes, modesty fled. She toed off her boots, unsnapped the pants and slid them down over her hips, hooking her bikinis on the way down.

Max's eyes followed her every move. He didn't seem to be breathing.

Raine wasn't sure she was, either, wasn't sure she needed to. Oxygen didn't seem nearly as important as chasing the sensations that flowed through her body like lava.

Naked, she stood for a moment, letting him look his fill, reveling in the tension that crackled between them. It lasted a moment. Two. Then he let out a low, reverent oath, crossed the room and took her.

That was how it felt, as though she were being *taken*. He swept her off her feet and carried her to the bed in an action that should have seemed foolish, but instead jammed her heart into her throat with excitement and an edge of fear that he might let her fall.

Then she realized it didn't matter.

She'd already fallen.

On that thought, on that hit of hot, wild desperation, she turned her lips into his neck and nipped the soft spot where his pulse pounded in time with hers. He murmured something—her name perhaps—and shifted her in his arms so he could take her lips with his, take her under again as they dropped to the bed, twined together.

She rose above Max, naked while he remained half-clothed. Then she paused. "Oh, hell. We don't have—"

He held up a finger. "Yes, we do. It's not all snacks and soda in that gift shop."

She grinned, bubbles of light froth and excitement expanding in her chest and bursting through her as she dropped from the bed, padded naked to the crinkling bag and extracted the small packet. Power spiraled through her. A sense of rightness.

This was right. No matter what came after, this was right for her. For them.

Riding on the high, she turned back with the thin box held between her thumb and forefinger. "You planning on a three-fer?"

She faltered when she saw that he was standing beside the bed, gloriously naked, supremely confident.

He was as heavily muscled and perfectly proportioned as she had imagined in her darkest, unacknowledged fantasies. But the whole of him was more than she'd pictured. More warrior-like. More masculine. And his proud, jutting flesh suggested that he was up for anything.

He held out a hand. "Come over here."

She hesitated briefly as nerves tangled with needs inside her, then crossed the room and pressed the condoms into his hand. "I was hoping we'd end up like this."

Part of her wished he'd say something about this being a beginning rather than an end, but no such assurance was forthcoming. Instead, he kissed her—a simple, closed-mouth kiss that quickly spiraled into something more, something larger than itself. Skin slid across skin, inciting delicious friction, torturous want.

She drew him down to the soft bed, or maybe he urged her down, she wasn't sure anymore whose idea was what, she only cared that the kisses didn't stop, the friction didn't stop.

The heat built. Quiet was forgotten; gentle was lost to the inferno of passion as they strained together, twined together, kissing and nipping until Raine's entire essence was steeped in him.

He said something on a low growl. The dark, almost violent sound of it pulled at her, inflamed her, called to something deep within her. She whispered his name in a demand, a plea, and parted her legs, wrapping them around him and rolling so they reversed to a position as old as humanity itself, with him atop her, his hard flesh nestled at the juncture between her legs.

The need pounded in her blood while he sheathed himself in one of the condoms and set the other two on the bedside table. Then he was back there with her, truly *with* her, focusing all his attention on her with a fierceness that might have been intimidating had she not trusted him.

But she trusted him. Hell, she loved him. So she opened to him, welcomed him, demanded him the way her body had been clamoring for his, ever since that first moment she'd knocked on his apartment door and been forcibly reminded of what she'd left behind in Boston.

At the time, she hadn't understood. Now, as he slid into her on one graceful thrust of hard against soft, flesh against flesh, she finally did understand.

When she'd run from her hospital room, she hadn't just left her job and a man who might have been her lover. She'd left a piece of herself behind. She might not have ever understood the enormity of it, the finality, except for one thing—

As he moved inside her, as he loved her, that piece was restored.

The beauty and power of it, the heat and the mad frenzy gripped her tightly. She might have struggled against the hold, except it was pulling her exactly where she wanted to be, down into the swirl of pleasure and sensation and flesh and Max, only Max, who waited for her at the center of it all.

Their eyes locked as surely as her legs gripped his hips and her hands anchored at his shoulders. She saw herself reflected in his dark irises, saw the flicker of candlelight and emotion. And heat. So much heat it nearly scorched her, burned through her like a nearing wildfire, increasing with every second.

Their bodies moved together with relentless rhythm, slowing down, then building as the sensations layered within her. But where always before Raine's climax had turned her inward, until she concentrated on that deepest core of herself, this time, the sensations radiated outward, encompassing Max, drawing him into her pleasure as it spiked and imploded, carrying her along with it.

No, she realized as her body pulsed and clenched around him and he groaned deep within his throat, within his soul as he emptied himself into her. The tidal wave of sensation wasn't carrying just her along with it this time. It was carrying *them.* Together.

The tide built and crested, then just when she thought the ebb was inevitable, Max moved in a long, slow glide of flesh against flesh. Raine cried out in surprised pleasure and tightened around him once again, wringing a groan from him. Her name perhaps, or a prayer.

As the sensations faded, as the dim light came into focus around them, Max collapsed gently atop her, pressing her into the yielding mattress with his good, strong weight.

He said her name. Pressed a kiss to her temple. And laced his fingers between hers and held on.

Then they lay there.
Together.

THEY TURNED TO EACH OTHER twice more as the snowstorm built, crested and then ebbed outside, leaving the world cloaked in white and the plow crews working double duty to keep the roads open.

The third time, they drew out the experience as long as they could.

If their first time together had been all need and greed, and their second time together had moved with the fresh, exciting rhythms of new lovers, then their third time was forever. Simply forever.

Though she hadn't said the words—and neither had he—Raine knew they'd made a commitment to each other that third time. They had soundlessly agreed to make a go of it, to find a halfway point between his desire for a homemaker and her desire to be a high-powered executive. Between trust and distrust. Between rescue and equality.

They'd find their compromises and make

them work. What they had together was too special to lose.

Afterward, they dozed, twined together, until Raine woke near dawn. She held herself still, listening to her own heartbeat. To his, where her cheek was pillowed on his chest.

Max slept the deep, motionless sleep of satiation. He didn't stir when she said his name. In fact, he barely appeared to be breathing.

It was foolish and feminine to be pleased by how thoroughly she'd undone him, but Raine felt both foolish and feminine, so that was okay.

Still, it was time for them to get up and out before their shot-up truck attracted attention.

Thinking to get a head start while he slept a bit longer, Raine levered herself away from him. Sitting cross-legged on the bed with one of the blankets draped over her shoulders against the morning chill, she watched him for a few seconds, memorizing the moment.

Though he slept deeply, his features weren't soft or any less forbidding in repose. He remained formidable, as though chiseled in stone.

But she knew the gentle warrior within.

She touched his shoulder, knowing there were demons yet for them to face. "Max. Time to get up."

He mumbled something and grabbed her hand, but didn't wake.

Her heart tugged at the pressure of his fingers on hers, and she bent and kissed him. "Fine. You sleep. I'll pack and check out."

As she mentally reviewed the smaller highways they could use on their trip back to Boston, she realized they would pass very near the burned-out wreck of her rental house in New Bridge. Max's truck should still be parked in the driveway. Did they dare switch out?

"Probably not," she murmured. "If The Nine aren't watching the house, you can bet Detective Marcus is."

And if anyone had told her a week earlier that she'd be avoiding the police with relative calm by the weekend, she would've called them a liar.

There was no doubt about it. She'd changed.

Maybe she'd finally grown up in her mid-thirties.

She clicked on the light in the bathroom and got herself dressed, figuring Max would wake with the commotion. She left his clothes and weapon out, along with the food and drinks they hadn't gotten to the night before, and packed everything else away in his duffel.

When there were still no signs of life from the bed, she shook his shoulder. "Come on, Max, wake up! What's the matter, did I wear you out?"

She flipped the clock radio on, cranked the volume, and said in a loud voice, "I'm going to check out and load the truck. If you're not up when I get back…" She let the threat hang, having no idea what she'd do.

He muttered and rolled over onto his back. Reassured that he'd soon be fully conscious, she pulled on his furry jacket liner, shouldered the heavy duffel, unchained the door and let herself out.

The hallway was several degrees cooler than the room. Raine shivered and huddled deeper in her borrowed coat. As the single elevator descended to the ground floor, she realized it felt strange to be alone. But there was no way for the shooters in the silver car to know where they were.

The outside air was ice cold and gloomy with the deadness of predawn. The parking lot was plowed and salted, but still slippery. Raine was shivering in earnest by the time she reached the truck, way in the back of the parking lot. She let the duffel slide off her shoulder and reached to stick the key in the driver's side door lock.

A footstep scraped on the sandy pavement behind her.

"That was quick," she said, her voice gaining a lilt at the thought Max had followed her out. "I thought you'd still be in bed when—"

She broke off at the click of a weapon and the feel of cold metal at her temple.

Her heart lunged into her throat and her guts dissolved to jelly. A whimper backed up in her throat.

Caught. She was caught.

"That's right, boss," a familiar voice said. "Behave, and neither of you will be hurt. Turn around, and keep your hands where I can see them."

She did as instructed, winding up with her back pressed against the side of the truck. "Jeff." Her voice broke at the sight of him. "How could you?"

Her once-trusted employee lifted one shoulder in his trademark half shrug, but there was no remorse in his blue eyes. "I've always been smart enough to find the shortcuts."

Behind him, a black limousine rolled to a stop. One dark tinted window buzzed down, and silver hair flashed within. The man Ike had identified as Dr. Frederic Forsythe stared out at Raine.

"Where are the disks?" Jeff said.

Though her gut churned with sick, greasy fear, she lifted her chin and glared at him. "How did you find us? We tossed the phone near where your boys crashed last night."

Jeff's chest expanded with pride. He nodded to the truck, with its shattered window and damaged dashboard. "A little something I've been working on for a while now. I did some of the initial work in your lab, come to think of it. I've created a homing device small enough to be easily implanted beneath the skin. Or, in this case, inside a bullet. But that doesn't answer my question." His voice dropped. "Where are the disks? The computer disk with the database information on it, and the video disk the lawyer stole. Tell us where they are. *Now.*"

He raised his weapon and leveled it at her right eye. The opening of the barrel was very, very black in the dawn light. It was Sunday morning. The realization brought a flash of stained glass and the quiet grace of a dead woman's memorial.

Too many people had died. This needed to end, now. But Raine was alone.

If you were planning on rescuing me,

now would be a good time, Max, she thought with growing desperation.

Impatience kindled in Forsythe's eyes. "Go find out what room they were in," the plastic surgeon finally snapped from the limo. "Bring Vasek out here. Maybe she'll be more cooperative once we put a bullet in him. There's no way we're leaving him alive. He's too damned dangerous."

"They both are," Jeff said. He glanced back over his shoulder at his boss. "We can't leave her alive to—"

"Shut up!" Forsythe said quickly, but not before she saw the truth in his eyes.

She and Max were both dead, regardless of whether they cooperated or not.

"Wait," she said, thinking fast. "What about a deal?"

Forsythe smirked. "You don't have anything I want."

"I have Thriller. I have the patents and the development rights."

"We've already taken care of your little drug." He lifted one shoulder, allowing her to see that he was elegantly and expensively clad even this early in the morning.

Or else he'd been waiting all night. He continued, "A pity. It would've made you a fair bit of money, but there was one major problem. It made women feel better about themselves. Sexier. More self-confident. Do you have any idea what that would do to the cosmetic surgery industry?" He shook his head. "No. It couldn't be allowed. So I dispensed poisoned samples to a few trusted associates and maneuvered things so suspicion would fall on you. Nothing personal—just an effort to confuse matters." His voice dropped. "Then that computer tech gave you a data disk that had the ghosts on it. Ghosts that could potentially be tracked back to me. That information could not be allowed to surface."

"So you decided to kill me." As the final missing pieces of their theory clicked into place, Raine forced herself not to react, instead putting herself back into the suddenly ill-fitting role of a woman who put career first, business first, success first. "That's not the only answer, you know." She jerked her chin at Jeff. "He'll tell you

I'm a career-minded woman. Let me go back to work on the formula. Tone it down a little. Tweak a benzene ring here and there until it works well enough to sell, but not so well that it's impacting your business. We can change the name, announce that we've fixed the problems we had with Thriller, and split the take. We're talking hundreds of millions of dollars here, and I've already done the hard part."

That got Forsythe's attention. He narrowed his eyes. "Why would you do that?"

"Because I'd rather be rich than dead," she snapped. "And because I'm a practical woman. An ambitious one. I want in. I want access to The Nine. Power. Success. All of it."

He stared at her as though judging her sincerity. As he did, the seconds ticked past beneath her skin.

Was Max coming out? Had Forsythe already sent other men in after him? How could she protect him? She had to think faster! What could she say to convince Forsythe?

Finally, the surgeon said, "How do I know you're serious?"

"I'll take you to the disks." She shrugged as though it didn't matter. "You can have them."

"Are they here?"

"No, they're someplace safe, up in Boston. I'll take you to where they're hidden—we've got it set up so only Max or I can retrieve them." She was lying through her teeth on that one, but brazened it out. "I'll hand them over as a gesture of good faith, but you've got to give me something in return. Otherwise, no deal."

"If you want me to leave the other woman alone, too late. We've already taken care of her. There was a tragic ferry accident on the crossing from the Cape to Nantucket." He tsked. "Such a shame."

Raine's heart constricted at Ike's fate, at the emphasis of just what a dangerous game she was playing. But she feigned a shrug. "She would've been a complication either way. No, I want you to let Vasek go free, unharmed."

Forsythe snorted. "Not a chance. If you

know about our little group, then so does lover boy. And he'll follow you, guaranteed. There's no way you can keep him from interfering."

"There is one way I can do exactly that," Raine said, pulse pounding with sick dread at what she was about to propose.

"How's that?"

"I'll break his heart."

Chapter Thirteen

Max awoke slowly when the lights came on, aware of the whole-body lassitude that came from good loving. His brain echoed with the words *I love you*. Had she said them, or had he merely thought them?

Either way, they were true.

He smiled and opened his eyes, then frowned when he realized the light wasn't coming from the hotel room lights, as he'd assumed. It was coming from the window. It was daylight, and the clock radio was blaring.

And Raine wasn't there.

She's in the bathroom, he told himself on a sudden spurt of panic. He craned his neck to see her, but the adjoining room was dark, the door ajar. No sounds came from within, no signs of life.

She went downstairs for coffee, he tried instead. But logic told him it was well past sunrise, well past the time they'd agreed to leave the hotel for Boston. *She's—*

Then he saw that his clothes were laid out beside the sodas and snacks.

And his duffel was gone.

"She didn't, did she?" He sat up in the bed, sick incredulity echoing in his head. "I didn't, did I?" He hadn't fallen for it again, hadn't trusted it again, had he?

He cursed, very much afraid that he had.

But where had she gone? Why? She still needed him to help build the case against The Nine.

Didn't she?

An awful suspicion struggled to form in Max's gut. He shoved it aside and climbed to his feet, cursing himself for having been exhausted, for having slept too deeply for far too long.

He dragged his clothes on and felt in the pockets of his jacket. "At least she left me the gun and the cash." The truck keys were gone, though, along with the duffel. He tried to find humor in the irony. "Cheaper to replace the bag than five rooms worth of furniture, at any rate."

But there was no humor to be had.

Fool me thrice and I'm an idiot, he thought on a burst of anger. He skipped the elevator, thundered down the stairs and shoved through a side door that dumped him straight into the parking lot.

The sight of the truck still parked in the far corner brought him up short. "What the heck?"

She'd taken the keys and left the truck? That didn't make any sense.

Instinct prickled along the back of his neck as he approached the vehicle. The morning sun had melted the snow to water, which held no tracks. There were a few fresh-looking scuffs in the salt scum that covered the side of the truck. Maybe a sign of a struggle. Maybe a sign that she'd tossed the duffel onto the hood and it had slid off.

When he reached the truck and looked

inside, he nearly sagged back at the gut-punch of emotion. Of anger.

The keys were in the ignition.

And a note lay on the seat.

He yanked the door open and grabbed the single sheet of paper. He was tempted to wad it up and throw it away unread, but some optimistic part of him wouldn't allow the gesture, just in case it was an explanation that meant something other than *gotcha.*

Dear Max, it began, wringing a snort from deep within his chest.

Go back to New York, the job is over. I'll wire payment from wherever Frederic and I wind up. You were right the first time—the plane tickets were mine. It was my idea in the beginning, everything except the dead women. I didn't sign up for that, which is why I ran, and why my so-called partners tried to kill me. There's no such thing as The Nine, that was all in poor Charlie's mind, though Frederic was one of my partners. When it came down to the wire, I just couldn't do it. I couldn't let the others hurt you. I love you— believe that if you believe anything. So I'm leaving. Let them have the drug. Tell Detective Marcus every- thing—it doesn't matter anymore. Regardless, we'll always have that night in Philadelphia.

She had signed it with her first initial.

I love you. The words danced on the page, mocking him. He cursed bitterly, wadded the paper and tossed it in a puddle of slushy water before he threw himself into the truck cab and cranked the engine. Then he cursed again, retrieved the note and flung the dripping mess into the foot well.

He drove to New Bridge, to her house, which was now nothing more than a deserted pile of blackened, charred rubble.

He left the ruined rental truck parked crosswise in the driveway and climbed into his own vehicle, figuring he and Detective Marcus would settle up later. Then he headed for the highway and took the west-bound ramp, headed for New York City.

Headed for home.

DURING THE THREE-HOUR RIDE into Boston, there was only silence in the limo passenger compartment. Raine stared out the window, unable to look at Jeff, unwilling to converse with Forsythe. The men worked on cell phone-connected laptops instead of talking to each other, maybe because she was there, or maybe because there was nothing to say until they reached Logan Airport.

Once they were on the circular, convoluted network of airport roadways, an intercom clicked on and the driver's voice said, "Which terminal, ma'am?"

"I don't know." Without conscious thought, she turned to Jeff. "Find out which terminal has a Thursday's Restaurant, will you?"

"Sure thing." He opened a new window on the laptop and tapped in a quick search. "Terminal B. Arrivals."

Forsythe chuckled. "Seems like she

trained you well, Jeffrey. You're still wired to jump at her command."

Jeff's face flushed a dull red and he glanced at Raine. She couldn't read his expression, but whatever was there, it didn't seem to be remorse. More like self-satisfaction.

"So, we're going to Thursday's, are we?" Forsythe glanced out the window, where jersey barriers signaled the edge of yet another construction zone. "Crummy little place. I hope for your sake the disks are there."

"They'll be there," she assured him, fingers crossed that Ike's care package included the database copy.

"And Vasek better *not* be there."

"No way. He's back in Manhattan by now, cursing my name." She forced a laugh, but worry was a sick coil in her stomach. What if he'd believed the note? What if the love she'd felt, the love she'd thought they'd shared, had all been on her side?

No, she told herself, he'd be there.

If he loved her, he'd trust her. If he

trusted her, he'd read the note carefully and grasp the buried clue. He'd come for her.

But what if he didn't come?

What if he didn't love her?

Forsythe sent her a long, measured look, but didn't press.

Moments later, the intercom went live and the driver's voice said, "Terminal B, Arrivals."

"Wait for us here," Forsythe ordered. "We won't be long." He waited for the driver to open the passenger doors, then gestured Jeff out first, followed by Raine. As she passed, Forsythe made a show of tucking a small handgun into the pocket of his wool coat. "For insurance purposes only, of course."

Too bad we don't have to go through security to get to Thursday's, Raine thought as she climbed out of the limo and stood shivering in the cutting wind coming off the ocean. With both Jeff and Forsythe carrying concealed weapons, they wouldn't make it three feet past the checkpoint.

Which was probably why Ike had chosen Thursday's. No doubt she walked around with a pistol strapped to her ankle on a daily basis.

Rather than bringing her down, the thought buoyed Raine. Ike was tough enough to survive, and she was as tough as Ike, damn it. She might not be wearing all black or packing heat, but she could pull this off.

Provided her backup, her *partner,* came through for her.

Come on, Max, she thought, the words nearly a prayer. *Give me the benefit of the doubt. Really* read *that note. Think about it with your heart, then with your head.*

And get your butt to the restaurant, or I'm in big trouble.

But there was no sign of him as Forsythe, Jeff and Raine entered Terminal B through baggage claim on the lower level and took an escalator up to the arrivals deck.

Sure enough, there was Thursday's Restaurant, in all its green-and-white striped glory.

A yawning pit opened up in the center of Raine's stomach. She didn't have a backup plan. What would she do if Max didn't show, or came too late? If she gave the disks to Forsythe, that would be the end of their efforts to gather evidence against The Nine, and it wasn't as if she would actually go through with her supposed alliance.

If they didn't kill her outright, they'd no doubt find a way to get her charged and convicted on the outstanding warrant.

Unless, she thought, scrambling madly for an idea. *What if I get Forsythe to pull his weapon in Logan Airport? That'd bring security. It wouldn't take care of the rest of The Nine, but it'd buy me some time. Buy us some time. I could—*

"You waiting for someone?" Forsythe inquired with a thread of steel in his voice. He moved up beside her and she felt the barrel of his gun dig into the point of her hip.

Panic licked past her defenses at the realization that he could put a bullet in her without removing the gun from his pocket, then disappear in the ensuing melee.

Even if he were caught, he'd already proven that he had friends in high places.

What had she been thinking? Raine looked toward the exit, instincts screaming for her to run. She couldn't do this, wasn't tough enough, wasn't smart enough, just wasn't enough.

Yes you are, partner. Max's imagined voice came out of nowhere, out of the little core of warmth in her midsection, the warmth he'd put there the night before. *You can do this.*

She took a breath and nodded to Forsythe and Jeff. "Okay, boys. Follow my lead." She marched into the restaurant, waved off the hostess's offer to seat them at a table and sat at the bar. Though it was barely 11:00 a.m., several of the other stools were occupied with travelers who either didn't think it was uncool to drink before noon or were in another time zone.

The bartender—late twenties, prominent Adam's apple—wandered over. "Get you something?"

"Gin and tonic with an olive, please."

Forsythe leaned close to her. "No funny stuff, Ms. Montgomery. We clear on that?"

She manufactured a haughty look.

"Same goes. We both know this could be a very good deal for your people. Don't mess it up for them."

He stared at her for a long minute before he nodded and leaned back. "Fair enough."

But his hand remained in his jacket pocket, which was roughly in line with her right kidney.

"Here you go." The bartender slid a glass in front of her. "Anything else?"

She frowned at the drink. "Where's the umbrella? This is supposed to come with an umbrella. What kind of a place is this, anyway?"

He nodded. "Of course, I'm very sorry for the oversight. One umbrella coming right up." He dropped down behind the bar, but instead of a brightly colored decoration, he came up with two sturdy envelopes. "Tell her hey from Rudy."

"Will do. Thanks, Rudy." Raine took the envelopes and nodded to Jeff, who was lurking behind Forsythe like a shadow. "Pay him for the drink and don't stiff him on the tip, will you, Jeffrey?"

She moved to open the first envelope,

but Forsythe took her arm and nudged her along with the hidden weapon. "We'll have a look at those in the limo, if you please."

Raine felt the walls closing in on her, felt her time count down and then expire as they left the restaurant. Crushing, over-whelming disappointment flooded her as they crossed the marbled lobby and headed for the escalators.

"Hold it right there, Ms. Montgomery. Mr. Forsythe. Police!" Detective Marcus suddenly appeared in front of her, flanked by a pair of airport cops. All three had their guns out and at the ready. Agent Bryce of the FDA stood behind them and off to one side.

Before Raine could process Marcus's appearance so far out of his jurisdiction, and Bryce's presence at all, Forsythe turned on her. "You set me up! Bitch!" He grabbed her, spun her around and clamped an arm around her throat. Then pulled his gun and pressed it to her temple. "Every-one stand back! Back! I mean it!"

Raine froze, panic congealing in her blood. Forsythe nudged her toward the escalator. "Start walking. You got me into this, you're going to get me out of it."

She stumbled, dragging on numb legs. Oh, God. Oh, help. Oh—

Max!

He appeared from behind a marble upright beside the escalator, lunged at them and knocked Forsythe away from Raine in a move that was part football tackle, part rage.

They went tumbling down the up escalator, triggering screams from startled tourists. Raine staggered and fell to her knees, then struggled up and ran toward where the man had disappeared. "Max. *Max!*"

They came back into view, rising on the ascending escalator. Max's eyes gleamed with battle lust, Forsythe's with rage as they struggled for possession of the gun.

Max bared his teeth and roared with the effort of forcing the weapon up, toward the ceiling. The gun fired once, twice, spending its bullets in the acoustic tiles far above.

Then Max slammed Forsythe's wrist

into the railing and the gun fell free. He grabbed Forsythe by the jacket collar, pinned him down and punched him once, twice, a third time before the escalator reached the top.

Security forces swarmed and grabbed both men.

"Enough!" Detective Marcus shouted. He shoved Raine aside when she would have run to the men and grabbed Max. "Stand down, Vasek. That's enough!"

"It's not nearly enough." Breathing heavily, Max glared at the plastic surgeon, whose carefully preserved face was beginning to balloon and turn an ugly shade of red. Then Max glanced at Marcus. "You get the other two?"

"Two?" Raine said. She looked over to where Jeff stood, cuffed and cowed. "There was another?"

"Nice try, Ms. Montgomery. We know you and Forsythe were in collusion." The detective looped her wrists in front of her and fastened a pair of handcuffs before she could react. As ice gathered in her gut, she heard him say, "I'm arresting you on an outstanding warrant. We'll figure out the other charges later." He Mirandized her and then glanced over at Max. "Thanks again for your help, Mr. Vasek. Agent Bryce and I will see that the evidence gets to the proper authorities."

A rushing noise built in Raine's ears, like the wind, only louder. She went utterly, completely still. "Max?"

He took a long, hard look at her, then turned away.

She screamed his name, but he didn't look back.

"This way, please, Ms. Montgomery." The detective marched her through the terminal, flanked by armed security guards. The cuffs and escort earned her black looks from everyone she passed, tourist and employee alike. Under any other circumstance, it would have made Raine feel like a criminal. A terrorist. A terrible person.

But now, she was numb, except for the screaming, tearing pain in her chest.

Max had come, but he hadn't trusted her.

"In here." The detective stopped at a

door marked Security Only and gestured for one of the uniformed men to open the door with a key card.

They urged Raine through, into what looked like four or five interconnected rooms with viewing glass between them and a central area. Interrogation.

Over the buzzing in her brain, in her soul, Raine said, "I'm not saying anything without my lawyer present."

The detective's voice softened. "Don't worry about it. I had my fingers crossed when I read you the Miranda warning, so it doesn't count anyway." His eyes warmed and he held up a key. "Give me those cuffs."

Raine gaped as he freed her. "What's going on?"

"A little subterfuge," said Max's voice behind her. "Just in case Forsythe's friends were watching."

MAX SAW HER TURN TOWARD HIM, saw her eyes widen. Then a huge, joyous, relieved smile split her face. "Max!"

They met halfway across the interrogation

holding area. There was no hesitation, no holding back.

This time it was right.

This time they trusted it.

He folded her in his arms and held her tight, then ran his hands over her body, assuring himself that she was there, she was safe. Overwhelming, pounding relief thundered through him, chasing away the terror of the past few hours and the adrenaline of the fight, where he would have killed Forsythe if Marcus had let him.

He buried his face in her hair and said her name. "Raine." Then again. "*Raine.* He didn't hurt you?" When she didn't answer immediately, he held her away from him and gave her a little shake. "Raine. Did he hurt you?"

"No. I'm not hurt." Tears glistened in her eyes, but they seemed born of the same emotion that clogged his throat now that it was all over, now that they were safe. Together. Her lips trembled to a smile. "You figured out the note."

"We'll always have that night in Philadelphia," he quoted. "Yeah, I got it."

He didn't tell her how close he'd come to not getting it, how close he'd come to making the biggest mistake of his life. A mistake that could have cost her life.

He'd been miles down the highway before he'd started to wonder what, precisely, he was supposed to remember about their night in Philly. They'd met with James Summerton. Raine had held the baby. They'd shared takeout, kissed and spent the night in separate beds. Hell of a way to spend a Thursday night, he'd thought as he'd driven away from her.

Moments later, he'd been banging an illegal U-turn across a police cut-through on I-95.

Now, he touched her cheek with the back of his hand, then framed her face with both hands, not quite convinced she was real, she was safe. "We spent Thursday night in Philly. Thursday night. Thursday's Restaurant. Good hint."

"Thank you for coming." She looped her fingers around his wrists so they were holding each other, staring into each other's eyes, and he could see the truth and the fear and the awful worry, each emotion echoing into his own gut. "Thank you for trusting me and believing I didn't run away from you this time."

"It was a toss-up for a few seconds there," he admitted, "but when I came down to it, only one thing really mattered."

"What?"

"You." He touched his lips to hers. "I love you. And loving you meant that I had to go against the evidence and history, and believe that you loved me back."

"I did," she whispered. "I do." She reached up and kissed him. "Everything else is negotiable. That part isn't."

Cheerfully ignoring the good-natured catcalls from airport security, Max took her in his arms and kissed her the way he'd wanted to from the first moment he'd seen her in Boston. Only now, he wasn't kissing a dream or a fantasy. He was kissing a real woman. One who loved him right back.

She was laughing when she pulled away. "I don't suppose this helps your Damsel In Distress Syndrome, though, because when it came right down to it, I needed you to rescue me."

He shrugged and touched his lips to hers. "You rescued me first. Let's call it even and go from here."

Her eyes darkened. "Where *do* we go from here?"

"Away," he said. "Someplace safe."

"You think The Nine will be after me." It wasn't a question.

"I think that's pretty much a given." He slid an arm around her shoulders and cuddled her to his side. "Ike is safe, though they hit the ferry she and her date should have been on. That and the evidence we've gathered will be enough to put Forsythe and Jeff away for a long time, and it should allow Agent Bryce and other federal agencies to open an investigation of The Nine. Turns out I was wrong about Bryce— he's not on their side, just not really a people person. William is going to help where he can, and Ike may do a little more digging." He looked down at her and braced himself to deliver the bad news. "You'll have to put Thriller on the back burner for a little while. We want them to believe you're still in custody. That'll buy the investigation some time."

When he paused and looked down at her, she tightened her grip on his wrists. "Going away sounds nice." She smiled and felt the acceptance echo deep in her soul. "Don't look so surprised. You're not the only one who's figured out a few things over the past week. I'm still committed to Rainey Days and Thriller, but other things are important, too. Like taking down The Nine. Like taking some time away with you. Preferably someplace warm."

He smiled at the glint in her eye. "It won't be so bad. Think of it as practice for our honeymoon."

She grinned so hard she nearly glowed. "It's a deal. And in between massages, umbrella-wearing drinks and dips in the pool, we can discuss a few important details."

"Such as?" he asked, figuring she was thinking of children and families, a major area where they'd have to meet halfway.

"Furniture." At his startled look, she

laughed. "If I'm moving Rainey Days to New York City, I'm not sleeping on the floor of your apartment, got it?"

He laughed as he drew her in for another long kiss. "Yeah, I got it."

He'd gotten the most important thing in the world.

Raine's love.

* * * * *

Don't miss Jessica Andersen's next gripping romantic suspense, featuring techno whiz Ike Rombout who may have finally met her match, coming in April 2007!

Happily ever after is just the beginning...

Turn the page for a sneak preview of
DANCING ON SUNDAY AFTERNOONS
by
Linda Cardillo

*Harlequin Everlasting—Every great love
has a story to tell.*™
*A brand-new line from Harlequin Books
launching this February!*

Prologue

Giulia D'Orazio
1983

I had two husbands—Paolo and Salvatore.

Salvatore and I were married for thirty-two years. I still live in the house he bought for us; I still sleep in our bed. All around me are the signs of our life together. My bedroom window looks out over the garden he planted. In the middle of the city, he coaxed tomatoes, peppers, zucchini—even grapes for his wine—out of the ground. On weekends, he used to drive up to his cousin's farm in Waterbury and bring back manure. In the winter, he wrapped the peach tree and the fig tree with rags and black rubber hoses against the cold, his massive, coarse hands gentling those trees as if they were his fragile-skinned babies. My neighbor, Dominic Grazza, does that for me now. My boys have no time for the garden.

In the front of the house, Salvatore planted roses. The roses I take care of myself. They are giant, cream-colored, fragrant. In the afternoons, I like to sit out on the porch with my coffee, protected from the eyes of the neighborhood by that curtain of flowers.

Salvatore died in this house thirty-five years ago. In the last months, he lay on the sofa in the parlor so he could be in the middle of everything. Except for the two oldest boys, all the children were still at home and we ate together every evening. Salvatore could see the dining room table from the sofa, and he could hear everything that was said. "I'm not dead, yet," he told me. "I want to know what's going on."

When my first grandchild, Cara, was born, we brought her to him, and he held her on his chest, stroking her tiny head. Sometimes they fell asleep together.

Over on the radiator cover in the corner of the parlor is the portrait Salvatore and I had taken on our twenty-fifth anniversary. This brooch I'm wearing today, with the diamonds—I'm wearing it in the photograph also—Salvatore gave it to me that day. Upstairs on my dresser is a jewelry box filled with necklaces and bracelets and earrings. All from Salvatore.

I am surrounded by the things Salvatore gave me, or did for me. But, God forgive me, as I lie alone now in my bed, it is Paolo I remember.

Paolo left me nothing. Nothing, that is, that my family, especially my sisters, thought had any value. No house. No diamonds. Not even a photograph.

But after he was gone, and I could catch my breath from the pain, I knew that I still had something. In the middle of the night,

I sat alone and held them in my hands, reading the words over and over until I heard his voice in my head. I had Paolo's letters.

* * * * *

Be sure to look for
DANCING ON SUNDAY AFTERNOONS
available January 30, 2007.
And look, too, for our other
Everlasting title available,
FALL FROM GRACE by Kristi Gold.

FALL FROM GRACE
is a deeply emotional story of what a
long-term love really means.
As Jack and Anne Morgan discover,
marriage vows can be broken—
but they can be mended, too.
And the memories of their marriage
have an unexpected power to bring back
a love that never really left....

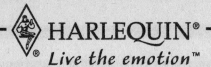

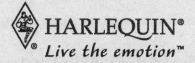

HARLEQUIN®
INTRIGUE®

BREATHTAKING ROMANTIC SUSPENSE

Shared dangers and passions lead to electrifying
romance and heart-stopping suspense!

Every month, you'll meet six new heroes
who are guaranteed to make your spine tingle
and your pulse pound. With them you'll enter
into the exciting world of Harlequin Intrigue—
where your life is on the line
and so is your heart!

THAT'S INTRIGUE—
ROMANTIC SUSPENSE
AT ITS BEST!

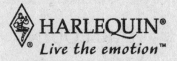

HARLEQUIN®
Live the emotion™

HARLEQUIN®
Presents

**The world's bestselling romance series...
The series that brings you your favorite authors,
month after month:**

Helen Bianchin...Emma Darcy
Lynne Graham...Penny Jordan
Miranda Lee...Sandra Marton
Anne Mather...Carole Mortimer
Susan Napier...Michelle Reid

and many more uniquely talented authors!

Wealthy, powerful, gorgeous men...
Women who have feelings just like your own...
The stories you love, set in exotic, glamorous locations...

HARLEQUIN®
Presents

Seduction and Passion Guaranteed!

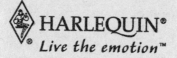